Parallel lines

Robert Rigby

About the author

Robert Rigby is best known for writing the bestselling *Boy Soldier* series with Andy McNab. He began his career as a journalist, then turned to writing for radio, television and the theatre and has also directed and performed in children's theatre throughout the country. He wrote the novelizations of the movies, *Goal!* and *Goal II*, and a third novel in the series, *Goal: Glory Days*. His scripts for television include the long-running BBC children's drama, *Byker Grove*.

ALSO IN THIS SERIES

Running in her shadow

Parallel lines

An official
London 2012 novel

Robert Rigby

CARLTON
BOOKS

First published by Carlton Books Limited 2011
Copyright © 2011 Carlton Books Limited

London 2012 emblems: ™ & ® The London Organising Committee of the Olympic Games
and Paralympic Games Ltd (LOCOG) 2007.
London 2012 Pictograms © LOCOG 2009. All rights reserved.

Carlton Books Limited, 20 Mortimer Street, London, W1T 3JW.

A CIP catalogue record for this book is available from the British Library.

10 9 8 7 6 5 4 3 2 1

ISBN: 978-1-84732-750-5

Printed in the UK by CPI Mackays, Chatham, ME5 8TD

FSC
MIX
Paper
FSC® C020471

One

It was muddy. Thick, dark, sticky mud, and that was just the way Sam liked it. Three days of pouring rain had soaked into the ground and the grass was cutting up under thirty pairs of boots, making it look more like a ploughed field than a rugby pitch.

The big forwards, their boots clogged and heavy, were finding the going tough. The lighter backs, whose shirts and shorts were weighed down by the driving rain, could hardly lift their feet to run.

But at the heart of the game and at the centre of the action, scrum-half, Sam, who was much lighter than the forwards, but stronger and more muscular than the backs, was having a great time and loving every minute. A lot depended on Sam. He was the captain and the best player in his school team.

The match was almost over. It had been fiercely fought, and after each side had scored a converted try and a penalty, the scores were level at ten points each. Now both teams were battling to the end, desperate for the win.

Crowds gathered along the touchlines. Pupils and teachers from both schools had braved the rain and were huddled together under a forest of umbrellas, shouting and cheering their support.

'Come on, Sam!' someone yelled. 'We can still win this!'

Sam believed this too. As far as he was concerned, a match was never won or lost until the final whistle sounded. And that was still a few minutes away.

It wasn't looking good, though. Sam's team had been on the defensive for the past ten minutes or more and several boys looked exhausted. They had just won a scrum, but it was dangerously close to their own try line.

Sam was holding the ball. He wiped it on his shirt and then his shorts, trying to clean off some of the mud and dry it a little so that he could get a better grip.

Steam rose from the two sets of panting forwards as they jostled together, breathing hard, their faces streaked with rain and mud. Wearily, they got down to form the scrum and then pushed, waiting for Sam to put the ball in.

He looked around the field and saw his backs stretched out in a line, ready to receive his pass and launch an attack. But Sam knew that if he got the put-in to the scrum wrong and the other team managed to snatch the ball, they could easily be in for a match-winning try of their own.

Sam crouched down, stared into the tunnel formed by the two locked-together opposing front rows, and then threw in the ball. It was a good put-in, and the ball was quickly heeled backward by Sam's teammate. It slithered through the scramble of boots and legs to the back of the scrum where it finally came to rest on the wet, dark mud.

Sam waited. Once he picked up the ball again, the opposing team could come charging forward and try to grab it. But not until then.

He glanced quickly to one side and then the other. His teammates stood ready, one long line stretching across the centre of the pitch, with a couple more players on the narrow, touchline side. They were all poised to make a break if he sent the ball in their direction.

It was up to Sam to make the decision.

Suddenly, he swooped down, grabbed the ball in both hands and made to pass it to the fly-half on his inside.

The opposition scrum-half came lunging towards him, but Sam didn't let go of the ball. Instead, he pulled it tight to his body and jinked to his left, sending the other scrum-half in the wrong direction. Sam kept low, the ball securely in both hands. He dodged another player coming in to tackle him and ducked under the flailing arms of yet another.

In an instant he was in free space, with most of the other team fooled by his swift, dodging movement.

He put his head down and ran, charging away from the forwards, racing towards the opposition try line. His own backs tore after him, ready for a pass if the ball came their way. At the same time, the opposition backs were giving chase, desperate to make a tackle before he could touch the ball down and score.

Sam crossed the halfway line and kept running. The mud was thickest and heaviest in the middle of the pitch so as a defender got near, Sam switched direction again and headed towards the corner. The defender was fast, but not fast enough.

Pupils and teachers from both schools yelled and screamed as Sam ran on and on.

'Come on, Sam!'

'Tackle him!'

'Go, Sam, go!'

'Get him! Bring him down!'

Sam had no intention of letting anyone bring him down.

There was only one opposition player still to outrun, but he was fast. He was almost alongside Sam. Both boys pounded on through the mud, panting for breath, legs aching, arms pumping.

The try line came closer and closer and the other boy dived, aiming for Sam's legs. His hands made contact, but Sam was as slippery as an eel. He jinked yet again and the boy went sprawling in the mud as

Sam made his own dive, skidding as he thumped the ball down over the line and into the mud for the try.

On the touchline, the supporters from Sam's school exploded into shouts and cheers. And a few minutes later, as the final whistle sounded, they did it all over again, splashing about happily as the rain continued to fall. Sam had done it; the school had snatched the victory.

'You played very well, Sam. Well done.'

'Thanks, sir,' Sam said with his usual cheerful smile as he emerged from the changing room. 'It was a great game I really enjoyed it.'

The school rugby coach, Mr Farrow, was looking highly delighted. 'There was a county rugby selector at the match today. I've just been chatting to him, and he was very impressed with you. I think you'll be hearing from the county soon about a trial.'

Sam hesitated for a moment before replying, his smile fading. 'That's ... that's great.'

Mr Farrow frowned. 'You don't seem very pleased. A place in the county team would be a great honour.'

'Yes, I know. It's just that...'

'Yes?'

'Sorry, sir. It would be great, really.'

'Well, try to look a little more happy about it,' Mr Farrow said, a little crossly. 'I'm sure you'll do the school proud if you get selected.' He nodded and walked away.

Sam Warder was a pupil at Waterlands School, a very old, independent school that sat in beautiful, wooded grounds in East Anglia.

The school and many of its ancient buildings had been on the same site for hundreds of years. Sam was a boarder, which meant that he lived there during the week and went home for some weekends and during holidays.

Sam's dad had also been a boarder at Waterlands when he was a boy. Back then, the school was only for boys, but for the past fifteen years it had opened its doors to girls. Most of the girls said that after four hundred years, it was about time too! And that wasn't the only change. There were new buildings and up-to-date facilities and teachers with new ideas. In recent years Waterlands had moved with the times and become much more modern.

One thing had never changed, though. And that was the school's passion for rugby. All sport was important at Waterlands, but rugby was the most important of all. It was almost a religion.

Sam loved rugby, but there was one sport that was even more important to him – and that was gymnastics.

Two

Sam was a natural acrobat. As a small child he had learned to climb and roll and tumble without being taught. He had wonderful balance and a great sense of rhythm and movement, so that as he grew older and started gymnastics training, he quickly developed fantastic skills.

He was a fearless gymnast, running and jumping and climbing where other youngsters wouldn't even walk. He learned a trick that soon became famous throughout his school; he would run straight at a wall and then up it for three strides before pushing into a backflip and landing safely on his feet. He never failed, and even though it looked difficult, it was easy for Sam. His friends were always asking him to do it, usually when the teachers weren't looking, although there were a few teachers who also secretly enjoyed Sam Warder's famous 'running-up-the-wall' trick.

But Sam wasn't just interested in tricks. He was a member of a top gymnastics club and was edging closer to a place in the GB junior squad.

There was just one problem, and that problem was rugby.

Much as Sam loved his second-favourite sport, he knew that rugby and gymnastics didn't go together well. But as far as his gymnastics coach was concerned, rugby and gymnastics should never go together at all. And the closer Sam got to selection for the national squad, the more concerned his coach became. He reckoned that in rugby Sam ran too much risk of picking up a serious injury that could put an end to his gymnastics career before it had properly begun.

This difficult situation had been on Sam's mind for some time and after the awkward conversation with Mr Farrow, he was thinking about it again as he made his way back to his boarding house. He went through the large front door and was congratulated on the win by a few more pupils as he climbed the stairs and walked towards the room he shared with three other boys.

Sam was popular at the school and even more popular because he was a star rugby player. Sometimes he wondered if he would remain quite so popular if ever he gave up rugby for gymnastics.

He reached his room at the end of the long corridor, pushed open the door and went inside. Two of his roommates were already there. They had both been at the match earlier but one boy gave Sam yet another cheer as he dumped his bag on the floor and fell onto his bed.

'Great try, Sam,' the boy said. 'Even I couldn't have scored a better one.'

Sam laughed. 'You probably would have, Ollie. I've been telling Mr Farrow for ages that it's about time he put you in the team.'

'He just doesn't recognise my talent,' Ollie said with a huge smile on his face. 'No one does.'

Ollie was Sam's best friend at school and quite a joker. But unfortunately, although Ollie dreamed of playing rugby for the school, he was actually pretty bad at it. And he knew it.

The other boy in the room was sitting at a desk where he was tapping away on a laptop. 'You wouldn't even make the girls team, Ollie,' he said, without looking up. 'You're a total loser.'

Sam and Ollie said nothing, knowing that it wasn't worth starting an argument with Felix. He was a decent rugby player, too, but had never quite made the school team. And that irritated him.

Felix was well known for saying exactly what he thought, even if it did hurt other people's feelings. He went back to staring at his laptop screen and Ollie shrugged his shoulders and winked at Sam. Ollie rarely let anything get him down, even unkind comments.

The door opened and the fourth roommate came in. 'Fantastic game, Sam,' he said. 'You won it for us.'

Jack was usually the quietest one of the four; he was quite shy and rarely had much to say. But like so many other pupils at the school, he loved rugby, even though he was no great player himself.

Sam smiled modestly. 'Thanks, Jack. I was lucky to slip through their forwards for the try.'

'That wasn't luck, it was skill and—'

Suddenly Felix snapped his laptop shut. 'Can we all just shut up about how brilliant Sam is?,' he snarled. 'He scored a try, that's all. One try. He didn't win the Rugby World Cup!' He pushed back his chair angrily and sent it flying. Without another word, he stormed from the room, slamming the door behind him.

Ollie raised his eyebrows and whistled softly. 'What an exit; very dramatic. He should have auditioned for the school play like me.'

Three

It was an exciting time to be a top-flight gymnast, especially as the countdown to the London 2012 Olympic Games was well under way.

British men and women had never stood so high in the world rankings, with several gymnasts aiming for medals – hopefully gold medals – at London 2012. The top stars, like world and European champion Beth Tweddle and world championship medallists Louis Smith and Daniel Purvis were an inspiration for Sam.

He watched their medal-winning performances on television, not just as a fan, but also as a fellow gymnast. He studied every move, every twist and turn, every tumble and spin, every leap and landing. And as he watched, he learned.

The British junior men's team included European champions and several were pushing for places in the senior squad. That was where Sam was hoping to make his breakthrough. As some of the leading juniors stepped up, he wanted to grab a place in the junior squad.

But the plan didn't stop there. Gymnasts must be sixteen to compete at senior level, so at fifteen, and with a year to go to London 2012, Sam could still snatch a place in the Olympic team. But to make his dream come true, Sam would have to be completely dedicated, work harder than ever, stay injury-free and, on top of all that, carve himself a very large slice of good luck.

But then there was rugby, and as Sam kept being reminded, rugby and gymnastics didn't go together. It was a problem and it had to be sorted, but how?

Right now, Sam was in the middle of an evening training session at his gymnastics club. Several young gymnasts were working on different apparatus as he went through a new routine on the parallel bars, with his coach Mike Thompson watching every move very closely.

The young gymnast swept through a series of swinging movements and holds, sometimes operating on one and sometimes both of the parallel bars – two side-by-side bars that stood two metres above floor level.

'Good,' Mike called as Sam moved effortlessly from a pike position up into a perfect handstand, one hand firmly gripping each bar. 'Now, hold it, and ... go.'

Mike nodded as Sam switched smoothly back into swinging movements, working towards the dismount, the important end to his routine. Swinging upward and over, he released the bars, but he landed slightly off-balance and took one small step forward. Sam steadied himself and then stepped back into his final position.

'Mmm, not bad,' said Mike. 'You didn't quite stick it, though, did you?'

Sam nodded his agreement, knowing he hadn't made a perfect landing. 'I was a bit too far forward coming into the dismount. I overbalanced.'

'Never mind,' Mike said. 'The routine was pretty good. Take a break and then we'll do some work on the high bar before we finish.'

Sam towelled himself down and wiped the chalk dust, which helped him keep a firm grip on the bars, from his hands. 'Pretty good' was not good enough.

He sat on a chair close to the floor-exercise area. Another gymnast was practising his routine, smoothly going through a series of difficult somersaults, twists and leaps on the large square mat.

Gymnastics was a tough and demanding sport, and Sam liked it that way. There were six different events – the floor exercise, the pommel horse, the rings, the vault, the parallel bars and the high bar – which meant that there was so much to learn and to master.

Mike sat on the seat next to Sam and together they watched the other gymnast complete his routine.

'He's looking good,' Mike said. 'You are, too. But there's a lot to do before the regionals.'

The regional championship was a vitally important event coming up soon. Success there could go a long way in helping Sam to make it into the Great Britain junior squad.

'Right,' Mike said, standing up. 'Let's get onto that high bar.'

Sam stood up and the aching muscles in his legs, arms and shoulders quickly reminded him of the work he had already put in that evening. He smiled, thinking that sometimes, rugby was easy compared to athletics.

Mike had been a gymnast himself and was the first to admit that although he was good, he wasn't anything special. But once he turned to coaching he quickly became one of the best.

As well as being a coach at the nearby gymnastics club, Mike was also a teacher at Sam's school – a science teacher. His arrival at the school had made gymnastics popular and several pupils, like Sam, had since become members of the club. Some took the sport seriously, while others did it for fun and fitness, but only Sam was top class. On training nights, they all travelled together to the club in a school minibus.

After training that evening, Mike drove them back to school as usual. Even after an evening of intense gymnastics training, the boys had only one topic of conversation – rugby.

They reached the school gates and Mike drove through and on to the parking place. The vehicle came to a standstill, he slid back a side door and the boys began to pour out.

'Night, sir,' the first boy out said. 'Thanks a lot.'

'Goodnight, lads,' Mike replied.

Sam was last to get out.

'Sam?'

He turned back. 'Yes, sir?' When they were at the club or at a competition, Sam called his teacher 'Mike' but for the rest of the time he was 'Mr Thompson' or 'sir'.

'A quick word before you go in.'

'Yes?'

'About rugby.'

'Oh, right,' Sam said. He knew what was coming.

'I've had another chat with Mr Farrow. I don't think we're ever going to see this the same way.'

'No, I don't think you will.'

'So it's down to you, Sam.'

'I know it is … but…'

The teacher sighed. 'Look, if gymnastics were a hobby, then I wouldn't worry, but you're aiming for the very top, the Olympic Games. And as far as I'm concerned, you just can't continue with rugby any more. It's too risky.'

Sam hesitated for a moment. 'But … well, I like rugby a lot and … I don't want to…' It wasn't easy to put his worries into words.

Mike wasn't so hesitant. 'And you don't want to let down your friends or the school, especially when you're the star player in the team?'

Sam was no show-off and he never boasted about how good he was at any sport. He felt his face start to redden. 'I wouldn't say that I was the star player. It's a team game and…'

'I've seen you play,' Mike interrupted. 'And you're very good, by far the best in the team. But we all have to make choices and this is an important one for you. If you were seriously injured through rugby – a broken leg or a wrist – it could put you out of gymnastics for months, or maybe for ever.'

'But I've never been injured playing rugby,' said Sam. 'Not seriously, anyway.'

'You've been lucky so far,' said Mike. 'Look, I'm sure that if you give up rugby there'll be a few moans and groans around the school, but they'll get over it quickly enough. And you standing down from the team will give someone else a chance.'

Sam didn't reply, but his thoughts were tumbling through his mind.

'I don't want to force you into this. No one does,' Mike said. 'It's up to you.'

Sam nodded. 'I know. And ... thanks.'

'Think about it,' Mike said, with a smile. 'Talk it through with your parents. And if you choose rugby, then fair enough. But rugby and gymnastics don't go together, not at the top level. So you need to make a decision, and very soon.'

Four

'Give up rugby? Are you crazy? You can't give up rugby!' said Felix.

It was Friday afternoon and Sam, like many other pupils, was going home for the weekend. He enjoyed being a boarder, but looked forward to seeing his family and spending time with his very best friend, Charlie, who lived nearby.

Sam wanted to talk through his dilemma over gymnastics and rugby with his parents and Charlie. He was going to ask them all for their opinion on what he should do.

But Sam had decided to mention the situation to his roommates before leaving for the weekend. And he was already thinking that perhaps he had made a mistake.

When he'd said, as casually as he could, that he might possibly give up rugby, the three other boys instantly stopped packing and stared. Rugby was the most important thing in the entire school. Why would anyone want to give it up?

'You can't!' Felix said again. 'If you give up rugby you'll be letting down the whole school.'

Ollie, as always, was ready to come to his friend's defence. 'You're not being fair, Felix. Sam would never let the school down, not if he could help it.'

'He can help it all right,' Felix snapped. 'And he should know by now that rugby comes first at this school, before gymnastics or any other sport.'

'But you only have to watch Sam play to know how important rugby is to him,' Ollie said, still sticking up for his friend.

'Not any more, obviously. He just doesn't care.'

'That's not true. He's in a difficult—'

'It's okay, Ollie,' Sam said. He turned to Felix. 'I do care about rugby and about the school. But if I get injured at rugby it could mean the end of my gymnastics career. And I want to get into the national squad, you know that.'

Felix stared furiously at Sam. 'It's all so easy for you, isn't it? Rugby, gymnastics ... you've never really had to try. Maybe if you had tried, like the rest of us, it would matter more.'

'But it does matter.'

'Or maybe the truth is that rugby scares you.'

The room went completely silent for a moment.

Sam glared at his roommate. 'I'm not scared, Felix,' he breathed, 'not on a rugby pitch or anywhere else.'

'Oh, I think you are,' Felix said menacingly. 'You don't want to get hurt, so it's easier to stick to a nice, safe sport like gymnastics, where there's no contact with anyone else.' He edged towards Sam as though he was ready to punch him. 'I think you're a wimp who doesn't deserve a place in the school team.'

Sam stepped forward, his fists clenched, but Ollie quickly jumped between the two boys. 'That's enough, you two. There's no point in falling out. We're all friends.'

Felix sneered. 'Friends? I don't think so.' He took a step back but then pointed at Sam. 'If he quits the rugby team, I'll never speak to him again. And I'll ask to be moved from this room. I don't want to share with a coward.'

Sam was breathing deeply. He was angry with Felix, but even more angry with himself. He should have thought more carefully before just blurting out that he was thinking of quitting. But it was too late now; the damage was done. 'I didn't say that I was definitely giving up rugby,' he said. 'Just that I might.' Then he turned away and went back to his packing.

'See what I mean?' Felix said to Ollie. 'He's not just scared of being hurt on the rugby pitch. He won't even stand up for himself now.'

Sam felt his anger rising again. But he knew how stupid it would be to start a fight, no matter how hard

Felix tried to push him into it. 'I told you,' he said, without looking back 'I'm not scared. Not of you or anyone else.'

Felix shrugged his shoulders and then turned to Jack, who was sitting on his bed. 'And what about you?' Felix said. 'Don't you have an opinion? What do you think of our so-called *friend*?'

Jack looked nervously from Felix to Ollie and then at Sam. He spoke quietly. 'I'd be very disappointed if Sam gave up rugby.'

Felix raised his eyebrows. '*Disappointed*? Is that all?'

'Yes,' Jack said softly. 'That's all.'

Five

It was good to be home.

Sam had turned the argument at school over and over in his mind for most of the journey back to Billericay in Essex. He was disappointed and upset. Sam didn't like falling out with anyone, especially his friends.

He didn't really blame Felix for getting so angry. Felix was like that. He said exactly what he thought and didn't worry about the consequences. At least you knew where you stood with him. Sam was hoping that when they got back to school, his hot-headed roommate would have calmed down so they could patch up their friendship. They usually did.

Sam was in his bedroom, happy to be surrounded by familiar things. The sporting posters on the walls, the medals and trophies on the bookshelves, even the old picture books he'd sat and read as a young child – they were all comforting and calming at that moment.

He smiled as he looked across at an old toy, which sat on the chest-of-drawers. A tin acrobat hung by his arms from a bar, supported by two upright poles. When a key was wound up, the clockwork acrobat would swing and turn over and over on the bar, his metal legs folding and flexing from the waist, almost like a real acrobat or a gymnast.

The battered toy was dented in places and its once bright paintwork was scratched and dulled. But it still worked. It had first belonged to Sam's dad when he was a boy and he had eventually passed it on to his young son. Sam had always treasured it; sometimes he thought it was the toy that had first sparked his love of gymnastics.

He reached over, picked up the toy and carefully turned the key until it was fully wound. Then he set it down and watched as the acrobat began his whirring routine. Sam had seen it countless times before, but it always made him smile. He sat back on his bed with his fingers linked behind his head and he watched the acrobat perform.

It really was good to be home, but at the back of Sam's mind was the familiar, niggling problem. He knew that as soon as he returned to school it had to be sorted out once and for all.

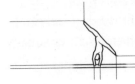

When all four members of the Warder family – Mr Warder, Mrs Warder, Sam and his ten-year-old sister, Emily – were at home, they always sat down together for their evening meal. It was the best time of the day, Mr Warder said, to talk and to share their news and their concerns. Sam had news and concerns on that first evening back at home, but he didn't rush to share either as the family enjoyed their meal.

Mr Warder worked for a large bank and was often away from home, travelling all over the world. Sam had no idea what his dad was like in his business life, but at home he was reserved and quiet. He was a good listener and Sam had often noticed that he never interrupted when someone else was speaking, always waiting until they finished.

Mrs Warder and Emily were the more chatty members of the family. Emily was delighted that her big brother was back for the weekend. Sam was her hero and she liked nothing more than showing him off to her friends.

'Liv and Chloe are coming round in the morning,' she told Sam between mouthfuls of food. 'You will be here, won't you?'

'I'm going to see Charlie at some point.'

His little sister frowned. 'What time, precisely?'

Sam smiled. 'I don't know what time, precisely. Maybe ten-thirty or eleven.'

'Okay,' his sister said. When Emily wanted to organise something she usually made it happen. 'Make it eleven-thirty, please. Liv and Chloe will be gone by then. And you wouldn't want to miss them, would you?'

'Oh, no,' Sam said, laughing. 'I definitely wouldn't want to miss Liv and Chloe.'

By the time the meal was almost over they had spoken about Sam's schoolwork and his friends and the talk was moving on to sport.

'Tell us about your gymnastics,' Sam's mum said.

'Yes please,' Emily added. 'I don't want to hear about rugby. It's too scary.'

'Really?' Sam said with a smile. His little sister had managed to bring the conversation to exactly where he wanted it without even trying. 'Well,' he said. 'There is a problem with gymnastics and rugby.'

His dad looked up from his dessert. 'Problem?' he said calmly. He put down his spoon. 'Then tell us about it.'

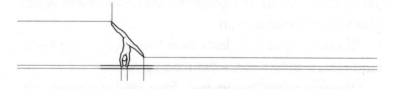

Sam and Charlie had been friends since their first day at primary school. They sat beside each other in their first classroom and as they grew older became the best of friends, partly due to their shared love of sport.

Then Charlie was badly injured in a car accident. He was in hospital for weeks and by the time he left, he knew that his damaged spine would never fully mend.

The boys' friendship grew even stronger. What Sam admired most about Charlie was that he never complained of his injuries or the fact that he now used a wheelchair. He was still a keen sportsman and had learned new skills, becoming a terrific table-tennis player.

On Saturday, they played a game at Charlie's house and, as usual, he was giving Sam the run-around, passing him time after time with a range of disguised spin shots, clever backhands and full-on smashes.

'Come on, Sam,' Charlie said as his topspin to one corner of the table beat Sam completely and left him swinging his bat at nothing but fresh air. 'You can do a bit better than that, can't you?'

'No, I can't,' Sam said, stooping to pick up the ball yet again. 'You're too good for me. You should have given me a five-shot start.'

Charlie laughed. 'I don't think five shots would have made much difference – I'm nine up, now.'

'Thanks for reminding me,' Sam said, throwing the ball back across the table. 'And yes, I do know it's match point.'

'Shall I give you an easy serve? One you can get back?'

Sam glared. 'No!' The two friends had always enjoyed their rivalry.

'Okay, you asked for it,' Charlie said with a shrug. He balanced the ball on the palm of his left hand, tossed it high into the air and sent a fast and low serve spinning across the net.

Sam lunged forward and just about got his bat to the ball, but the weak contact only pushed it into the net.

'My match,' Charlie grinned. 'Want to try again?'

'No, thanks,' Sam said. 'It's no contest when I play you.' He put his bat down on the table, grabbed a chair and went to sit next to his friend. He'd begun to tell Charlie about his dilemma earlier, but put it on hold for their game of table tennis. Now the worried look had returned to Sam's face.

Charlie spotted it instantly. 'So, tell me what your parents said about rugby and gymnastics.'

'They listened and then we talked for ages,' Sam said with a sigh. 'I told them everything, except for the bit about the argument with the guy in my room. I didn't want them to worry about that. In the end, though, they both said it had to be my decision. Only I can decide what's best for me.'

'They're right,' Charlie said, nodding. 'I know it's a tough decision – I wouldn't want to have to make it.'

'So you're not going to tell me what to do, either?'

'I can't, Sam,' Charlie sighed. 'No one can.'

Sam stared out of the window. 'Okay,' he said at last. 'I've been thinking it through for so long, weighing everything up, thinking about what I really want.'

'And?'

'And I've finally made my decision.'

'And?'

Sam got up, walked round to the other side of the table and picked up his bat. 'One more game, first. And this time I'll beat you.'

Charlie grinned. 'Ten-shot start? And you can serve.'

Six

The rumour had already spread around the school. It seemed to be on everyone's lips. From the moment Sam got back on Sunday evening he noticed people staring at him or whispering to each other as he passed.

Before he even climbed the stairs to his room an older boy he hardly knew stopped him in the corridor. 'Is what I've heard true?'

'I don't know what you've heard,' Sam replied. 'So how do I know if it's true?'

'I've heard that you're giving up playing rugby for the school team because you're scared of being hurt.'

Sam breathed heavily and felt himself blushing. 'I am *not* scared of being hurt,' he said, pushing past the boy and walking away.

The other boy called after him. 'We don't like cowards in this school.'

Sam almost turned back but he carried on to his room.

Ollie was there alone. 'Hi, Sam,' he said, his smile forced. 'Good weekend?'

Sam threw down his bag and sat on his bed, staring gloomily at the floor. 'Have you heard the rumour?'

Ollie came over and perched beside him.

'Everyone's talking about it.'

'You didn't start the rumour, did you?' Sam snapped, regretting the words the moment they left his mouth. He looked up and saw the hurt look on his friend's face. 'I shouldn't have said that.'

'No, you shouldn't,' Ollie said, softly.

'I know you didn't say anything,' Sam added quickly, 'and I know you wouldn't. And I really am sorry; all this is getting me down. It's been on my mind all weekend.'

'Forget it,' Ollie said, his smile returning. 'Did you say anything to anyone else before you left here on Friday?'

'No one.'

'Then it must have been Felix or Jack. But they're our friends, why would they do it?'

'I can't really blame whoever it was,' Sam said with a shrug of his broad shoulders. 'Anything connected to rugby is big news in this school.'

Ollie's smile suddenly changed to a look of concern. 'And I'm afraid I've got some more news for you.'

'What's that?'

I bumped into Mr Farrow when I got back. He said to tell you that he wants to see you in his office.'

'When?'

'Now.'

'But it's Sunday evening.'

Ollie shrugged his shoulders. 'He must think it's important.'

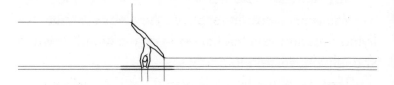

'Sit down, Sam.'

Mr Farrow glanced down at the sheet of notepaper on his desk and continued writing as Sam took the chair opposite and waited.

The office walls were covered with reminders of the school's great rugby tradition. There were framed photographs of teams from years gone by and more of young players pictured in action. There were framed Waterlands rugby shirts and shirts from famous clubs. There were even international shirts.

Eventually, Mr Farrow put down his pen and looked up. 'I've been working on the team selection for this week's match. There are a couple of injuries in the forwards so I'll need to make changes there.'

'Yes, sir,' Sam said, not sure at that moment what else he was meant to say.

'Is there something you want to tell me? About another change I might have to make?'

Sam swallowed. The rugby coach wasn't making this easy for him. 'I was going to come and see you; tomorrow.'

'Is that so?'

'Yes, sir' Sam said again.

'You know that there have been various rumours flying around the school since Friday afternoon, when you left to go home for the weekend?'

'That was my fault. I mentioned something ... something I was thinking about, to a few of my friends. I shouldn't have said anything until I got back.'

'Probably not,' Mr Farrow said. He didn't look very happy. 'So, after hearing these rumours for myself, and as you weren't here to answer them, I decided I should speak to Mr Thompson. He and I have had several conversations in the past about you giving up your place in the school rugby team.'

Sam nodded. 'Yes, sir, I know.'

'Because you *might* pick up an injury that could affect your future as a gymnast.' Mr Farrow stood up and went over to the window, which overlooked the school playing fields and the rugby pitches. It was dark outside, but the coach stared out as though he could see all the way down to the pitches.

'A lot of fine rugby players have been on those pitches, Sam.' He glanced back briefly at the framed rugby shirts. 'Some of them went on to represent their country, and some of them also played other sports, like cricket and athletics.' He turned from the window to look directly at Sam. 'I don't remember a single one of them giving up rugby because they feared they might get injured.'

'No, sir.'

'And what about you?'

Sam took a deep breath. 'I've thought about it a lot. I talked it over with my parents and with my best friend back home.'

'And what did they advise?'

'They didn't advise, sir. They said it was my decision.'

Mr Farrow nodded. 'And have you now reached a decision?'

'Yes, I have.'

Mr Farrow waited.

'I love rugby,' Sam said at last. 'I love being involved, being part of the team. And I love playing for the school and I know how important rugby is to everyone here at Waterlands.'

'In some ways rugby is the school, Sam,' Mr Farrow said. 'Many of our pupils came to Waterlands *because* of rugby.'

'I know. But I also love gymnastics. And my dream is to represent my country at the Olympic Games, maybe London 2012 or maybe the one after. I'm going to do everything I can to get there and I can't let anything get in the way. And that's why...'

His voice trailed away.

'Yes?'

'That's why I am going to give up rugby, sir.'

Seven

The gymnasium was a new addition to the school and although it couldn't compete with the gymnastics club and its full range of apparatus, it did have some top-of-the-range equipment, including a vaulting table.

Sam was working in the gym with the coach, Mike, early the following morning. One of the benefits of boarding school was that Sam was allowed training sessions before lessons started and after school. It meant that he could train twice a day, every day.

Often they used the gym for weight training or muscle-building exercises, saving the apparatus work for when they were at the club, but with an important competition quickly approaching, Mike had decided they should spend as much time as they could practising with the equipment. The vault was something they could work on at school. They had everything they needed: run-up mat, springboard, vaulting table and proper landing mats.

Sam stood at the end of the runway, trying to focus on every aspect of the vault, from run-up to landing. The vault itself would be completed in less than a second, but Sam knew very well that like all of the other gymnastic disciplines, it needed all his skill, speed, strength and power. And total focus.

He pictured the vault in his mind one last time. This particular one had a high 'start' value, which was another way of saying that it was difficult. They had been working on it for some time and Sam was gaining in confidence with each attempt. If he got it right in a competition, he would score very good marks.

Sam began to run, powering down the runway, arms swinging high to help him gain extra lift when he reached the springboard.

Mike watched slightly anxiously, seeing the fixed and determined look on Sam's face.

The young gymnast hit the springboard at full speed, both arms made contact with the vault table for a split-second and Sam soared high into the air, his knees tucked into his body as he turned over and over before landing, facing the table.

But he didn't quite stick it and found himself taking a couple of awkward steps backward, just about stopping himself from falling over.

'No!' he yelled angrily. 'That was a rubbish landing. I'll do it again.'

'Wait,' Mike said quickly.

'But I got it wrong.'

'Wait!'

Sam breathed heavily, totally frustrated with himself.

'Sit down for a minute,' Mike said.

'But...'

'Sit down.' Mike's voice was firm.

Sam perched himself on the edge of the landing mats and Mike sat next to him.

'There is such a thing as trying a bit too hard, you know,' the coach said.

Sam looked confused. 'But I thought...'

'We need the power, but we also need you to be relaxed going into the vault. You were tense and taut from the moment you started your run-up. The judges would spot that.'

Sam thought for a moment and then nodded. 'Yeah, I suppose I was a bit tense. Shall I go again now?'

'Listen, Sam,' Mike said. 'It's been a difficult few days for you, but you've made your decision. I'm delighted, obviously, but there are people in the school who are not so happy. They might see it differently when you turn up here one day with an Olympic medal.'

Sam smiled.

'But right now,' Mike said, 'you don't have anything to prove.'

'I ... I don't understand,' Sam said, feeling confused.

'Well, there's no point in giving up rugby to avoid a possible injury and then injuring yourself in the gym, is there? You have to be totally focused.'

'But I am, aren't I?'

'Not this morning. And, on top of that, you mustn't think you've got to justify your decision and prove yourself by trying too hard. You have to be relaxed, in your mind and in your body. Otherwise you'll end up injured. It's the same in any sport, you know that.'

Sam did know that what Mike said was perfectly true. And he realised at that moment that he had been feeling anxious since even before the training session began. The tension had been there as soon as he woke up. 'You're right,' he said. 'It is still on my mind.'

'Want to tell me what happened with Mr Farrow?' Mike asked kindly. 'It might help clear your mind.'

Sam nodded. 'He was pretty good about it, really. He was disappointed but said that he had to accept my decision and wouldn't try to change my mind. He even wished me good luck with my gymnastics.'

'And what about your friends?'

Sam shook his head. 'Not so good. Ollie's fine, but Felix, my roommate ... well, he's not my number-one fan right now. He says that he's asking to be moved to another room. He doesn't want to share with a coward.'

'That's unfair. You're not a coward, far from it. It takes bravery to make a decision like this.'

Sam shrugged. 'Not according to Felix.'

'And what about your classmates? Friends?'

'I haven't seen many others yet. But those I have seen didn't look too happy.'

Mike thought for a few moments. 'There's a school rugby match this week, isn't there?'

'On Friday afternoon,' Sam said, nodding.

'And should we win, even without Sam Warder at scrum-half?'

Sam laughed. 'We beat them easily last year, by about twenty points I think. They're not the toughest of opponents.'

'Good,' Mike said. 'A victory on Friday and all this will start to blow over. A couple more wins after that and everyone will have forgotten that you ever played rugby. They'll have a new hero to cheer on.'

'Good,' Sam said. 'Shall I do the vault now?'

Eight

The Waterlands team looked very different without Sam and the two injured forwards. Mr Farrow had made changes, but even though his team was in the lead, his players were not working well together.

There were fumbles, dropped balls, missed tackles and passes that went nowhere, or worse than that, straight into the hands of an opposing player. And the visitors seemed to have fielded a much stronger team than last year. All in all, the match wasn't proving to be anywhere near as easy as many had expected.

Sam had considered not turning out to watch, thinking that maybe some of his schoolmates would be angered to see him there as a spectator, but Ollie talked him into going.

'You have to be there,' he said firmly. 'If you're not, everyone will think you're hiding because you're ashamed of your decision.'

'But I'm not ashamed of my decision,'

'I know that.' Ollie smiled. 'So let's go, then.'

Now, they were on the touchline, standing slightly away from a larger group of spectators. None of them were enjoying it. And some of the spectators, including Jack, had been casting unfriendly glances in their direction.

Felix was on the pitch, playing his long-awaited first match for Waterlands.

Mr Farrow had reshuffled his backs. One of the centres had gone into Sam's position at scrum-half and Felix had come in to fill the vacant slot at centre. So far, though, he wasn't putting in a star performance.

The ball came out from a scrum and the new scrum-half passed it quickly to the fly-half by his side. It was a good attacking position and the backs began to pick up speed as they made their run.

The fly-half sent a long, spinning pass to the inside centre who in turn passed it on towards Felix. It wasn't a difficult pass and there was plenty of time to take the ball. But somehow Felix fumbled, knocking the ball forward so that it fell to the ground.

Most of the crowd groaned in dismay as the referee's whistle sounded for the knock-on and the game came to a halt.

Felix stood red-faced, staring down at the muddy grass. His clumsy mistake had lost Waterlands the chance of a much-needed try.

'He should have taken that pass,' Ollie muttered to Sam. 'Even I could have taken that one.'

'It's not easy in your first match,' Sam said. 'He's waited a long time for this chance and he's been playing quite well up until now.'

'No, he hasn't. He's been awful,' Ollie said.

Sam sighed, wishing that Felix would suddenly make a spectacular weaving run, ending in a wonderful try. But right now that looked unlikely: the newest member of the team was a bundle of nerves.

'Come on, Felix!' someone yelled.

'Show them we don't need that coward, Warder!'

Many of the crowd standing close to Sam and Ollie turned to look in their direction.

'Ignore it,' Ollie said to his friend.

But it wasn't easy for Sam to ignore the hurtful comment. He wondered if maybe it had been a mistake to come to the match after all. But he wasn't going to walk away now; that would make the situation worse.

From a scrum close to the halfway line, the opposition team began to make ground. Slowly but steadily, the big, burly forwards advanced.

'Hold them!'

'Keep them out!'

But the heavy forwards, working solidly together to protect the ball, edged closer and closer to the try line.

'Where are you, defence?'

'Hold them!'

'And watch for the breakaway!'

The shouts and yells from the touchline became more and more desperate as the defending players scrambled around, battling to grab back the ball. The shouted warning of a breakaway move went unheard.

Suddenly, the opposition scrum-half threw the ball wide. One of his teammates snatched it from the air, cleverly avoided a desperate tackle, then broke free into clear space.

In an instant he was away and heading swiftly towards the line. Only one player stood in his way. And that player was Felix.

'Grab him, Felix!'

'Bring him down!'

'Felix, tackle!'

Felix hesitated, frozen to the spot, his eyes wide and staring. Then at the very last moment he dived into the tackle.

The charging player simply jinked to one side and ran on unchallenged to touch down the ball between the posts for a try.

Felix was left sprawling on the ground, his hands over his head.

The scores were level and the other school's supporters went wild, cheering and shouting for joy on the touchline.

All around Sam, the stares and the glares grew even more hostile.

A girl from Sam's class stomped over. 'This is your fault,' she snapped furiously. 'Poor Felix is going to be blamed if we lose now, but it's all *your* fault. I'll never forgive you.'

'Sophie…' Sam said. But the girl turned and marched angrily away.

And then, while Sam was still reeling from Sophie's cutting words, a tall boy broke away from the group nearby and walked over to Sam, his eyes glaring.

'What do you want, Nick?' Sam said at last.

The other boy glared at him. 'Someone called you a coward earlier, Warder. Did you hear it?'

Everyone nearby was staring at them.

'Yes, I heard it.'

'Good, because it was me. I called you a coward. And I wouldn't want you to think that I was a coward, too – I'm not afraid of saying what I think to your face. What are you going to do about it?'

Ollie was looking worried. 'Do you want to leave?'

Sam shook his head. 'No, I'm staying till the end.' He turned back to the older boy. 'I'm not going to do anything about it. You're entitled to your opinion and I'm just here to watch the match.'

Nick sneered and turned away, while back on the pitch the ball sailed between the upright posts as the try was converted. Two more points were added to the visitors' score, putting them ahead for the first time.

And it didn't improve. Although the home side battled until the end, the scores remained the same. The visitors were victorious. Waterlands had lost a match that everyone believed would have been won had Sam Warder been on the pitch.

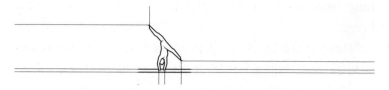

The mood in the room was dark and threatening, almost as though a storm was about to break.

They were all there: Sam, Ollie, Felix and Jack. And three hours after the end of the match, everyone was still shocked by the defeat.

Sam wanted to offer Felix some words of comfort, but he said nothing, knowing that nothing he could say would be welcome.

The silence drifted on and on. No one knew what to say.

Finally, Felix spoke. 'I had a terrible match,' he growled, more as an announcement to the whole room than to anyone in particular.

The three other boys looked at him.

'The nerves got to me, I couldn't handle it.'

'It's not your fault,' Jack said, for once speaking up quickly.

'Shut up, Jack,' Felix snapped.

Jack took a deep breath but remained silent as Felix turned his stare towards Sam.

'I asked to be moved from this room because I don't want to share with you any more,' he said. 'But I'm still here because I was told that this is a school and not a hotel.'

Despite the tension, Ollie, who tried to see the funny side of most things, couldn't stop himself from laughing. 'That's true enough,' he said. 'It's a pity it's not a bit more like a hotel, though. Room service would be nice.' His smile quickly disappeared as he spotted Felix glaring in his direction.

'Sorry, Felix,' he muttered.

Felix ignored Ollie and turned back to Sam. 'I don't blame you for what happened on the pitch today. I had my chance and I didn't take it. No one else can be blamed for that.'

Sam was desperate to say how sorry he was that it hadn't worked out for Felix, that he was certain it would be better next time, that Felix would feel more at home in the school rugby shirt, that nerves wouldn't affect him so much. But he stayed silent, knowing that nothing he could say would make him feel better.

Felix went on. 'You quitting gave me my chance.

But I still say that you should never have quit the school team, not for gymnastics nor for any other reason. It's a great honour to play for our school. I felt that today, even though I played like a beginner. And I let myself down.'

This time Sam had to speak. 'You *didn't* let yourself down!'

'I did!' Felix growled. 'I know that better than anyone. So, even though I've got to share this room with you for this year at least, I want you to know that our friendship is over. Finished. For good.'

There was no point in arguing with him, Sam knew that. Felix turned away and Sam stared miserably at the floor.

Ollie was trying to think of something – *anything* – that might help to somehow bring the two former friends back together. He looked over at Jack, hoping that perhaps he might come to his aid. But to Ollie's dismay, Jack got up and left the room without a word.

Nine

Sam's mobile phone was switched to silent. It was in his inside jacket pocket and as he and Ollie walked towards the school dining hall, Sam glanced anxiously at his friend as he felt the familiar vibration. Another text had arrived.

They weren't really meant to have their mobiles switched on during the school day, but many pupils did. Most teachers tolerated this unless the phones appeared during lessons.

But for the past few days Sam had kept his phone on almost constantly, and for a particular reason.

He and Ollie stopped walking and Sam took the phone from his pocket and pressed the button to display the text. Just like the others he'd received over the past few days, it was from an unknown number.

'Same number again,' he said to Ollie before reading the text.

> **Who the hell do u think u r? Special? No way! Youre a LOSER n a COWARD n u r gonna b SO SO SORRY!!!!!!!!**

Sam's face set hard as he passed the phone to his friend.

Ollie quickly read the message. 'Who's doing this to you?' he said, looking up. 'It's disgusting. We ought to report it.'

'No,' Sam said. 'I'm ignoring it, just like the comments at the match. I'm not giving whoever it is the satisfaction of thinking they've got me worried.'

'But you are worried, I can see that. And so am I. How many is it you've had now?'

Sam shrugged. 'I dunno. Ten, maybe.'

'It's a lot more than that, Sam. Twenty? Twenty-five? And that's in just three days. And what about all the texts you haven't told me about?'

'Whoever it is will get fed up soon,' Sam said. 'He's bound to, specially if I don't respond.'

'We don't even know if it is a "he". It could just as easily be a girl.'

'Maybe,' Sam said. 'I hadn't thought of that.'

'I have,' Ollie said quickly. 'I've been thinking of almost nothing else for the past few days, trying to work out who could be this … *sick.*' He paused for a moment before continuing. 'I don't like to say this, but … well, there is one obvious suspect.'

'You mean Felix?'

Ollie nodded.

'I don't believe it. We were friends.'

'Exactly, you *were* friends,' Ollie said. 'He's made it clear what he thinks of you now.'

'But I just don't believe he'd do something like this,' Sam said, taking back the phone and reading the text for a second time.

'We could ask him?'

'No,' Sam said. He stared at his phone. 'If only I recognised the number…'

'But you don't, and you won't,' Ollie said. 'That's the whole point.'

'What d'you mean?'

Ollie was usually one of the sunniest people in the whole school, but he looked very serious and worried at that moment. 'You've sent texts back to the number. No reply. He—'

'Or she,' Sam interrupted.

'Yes, all right, or *she*. Whoever it is will only text whenever he or she wants to. He or she…'

'Let's just call him "he" for now, shall we?' Sam said, smiling.

But Ollie looked grim. 'This is serious, Sam.'

'Yeah, sorry.'

'Okay, *he* has probably bought a new SIM card. They're cheap enough, and if he doesn't give out the number, then how will anyone know who it is? And he's using this phone number for one reason only: to send you threatening texts without giving away his identity.'

'They're not that threatening.'

'Oh, no? "You are gonna be so, so sorry",' Ollie said, reminding his friend of the last text message. 'What does that mean, then?'

Sam looked at his phone once more and then deleted the message. 'Whatever it means, it's gone now.'

Ollie sighed. 'It's easy enough to delete the texts,' he said. 'But you can't delete the problem quite so easily.'

Ten

Extra training sessions in the morning and after school, plus twice-weekly trips to the gymnastics club meant that Sam often had to catch up with his schoolwork while other boarders took time out to relax.

One evening, he was alone in his room working on a history project due in the following morning. Sam was quite pleased that two of his three roommates were elsewhere. The atmosphere when Felix was around was still frosty, with no sign of any improvement. And when Jack was in the room he was his usual quiet self, with not much to say about anything.

Ollie was out at rehearsals. As well at being a natural comedian, he was also a big drama fan, and his acting ability had won him a starring role in the production being staged at the end of term.

The play was based on the stories of the famous fictional detective, Sherlock Holmes, and Ollie was playing the great man's friend and assistant, Dr Watson. He was taking his role very seriously and between rehearsals spent much of his time entertaining his friends with a selection of Dr Watson's lines from the play.

Before leaving for rehearsals, Ollie had told Sam that he, or rather Dr Watson, would be back on the case to discover the identity of the mystery text sender as soon as he returned.

Sam laughed and told him not to worry, as he certainly wasn't bothered by what was going on. But that wasn't exactly true. There had been many more nasty texts, and they were beginning to get him down.

But concentrating on his work now was at least giving Sam something else to think about. He was researching on the Internet, searching for answers he needed, when a ping from his laptop told him that someone wanted to chat online.

Without stopping to think, Sam accepted the request. He spotted immediately that it had come from a user with an untraceable address.

Sam stared at the screen and waited. His mouth went dry when he saw the words that appeared on his screen.

REVENGER: Hello Loser, wanna chat...?

Sam stared in disbelief. Loser was the name the mystery text sender called Sam in his messages. He waited, his eyes fixed on the screen, not daring to respond. The curser blinked and then more words appeared.

REVENGER: Wots wrong, Loser? Got nothing to say? Wanna chat about being a coward? Thought youd have plenty to say bout that!

Sam's eyes blazed. His hands went to the keyboard and he furiously typed in his reply.

SAM WDR: Who r u???

Sam could almost hear the mocking laughter as his tormentor sent his own response.

REVENGER: Ur worst nightmare.

SAM WDR: Felix?

REVENGER: Wouldn't u like 2 no!!!!!!!!!!

SAM WDR: Wot do u want? Why are you doing this?

REVENGER: Because u r a coward. And u let us down. And u r gonna b so so sorry 4 wot u did.

SAM WDR: Ur the coward.

REVENGER: No, I'm the REVENGER. As u will c. Don't u feel ashamed LOSER? For letting every1 down???

SAM WDR: I didn't. I just made a decision.

REVENGER: Bad decision, LOSER. And wrong!!!!!!!

SAM WDR: Who r u?

REVENGER: I told u who I am. Got 2 go now.

SAM WDR: No, wait. Let's talk. We can sort this out.

REVENGER: I'll b back. U'll see. C u soon LOSER...

Eleven

Today was a big day and although Sam couldn't forget the threatening messages, he had to somehow lock them away at the back of his mind.

A vitally important competition was taking place and he had to be totally focused. An outstanding performance at the regional championships might even gain him his longed for first call-up to the national junior squad.

Sam knew he was at peak fitness and physically ready for the competition. But his mind had been in turmoil for days. And even though there had been no more online contact, the barrage of threatening texts had continued.

Night after night, Sam had stayed awake, trying to work out who was sending the messages. He found himself staring at his friends, and his former friends, becoming suspicious of people he knew for certain wouldn't possibly do such a thing. Or would they? He just didn't know any more.

And the texts kept coming; the most recent had arrived that morning as Sam was changing for the competition.

His heart started to thump as soon as he heard his mobile buzz. He wanted to ignore it, but he couldn't.

> **Hi LOSER, big day 2day.**
> **I'll b thinking of u.**
> **U will LOSE because**
> **u r a LOSER!!!!!!!!!!!**

Sam deleted the text immediately and angrily switched off the phone and shoved it back into his coat pocket. As he warmed up in the sports hall and prepared for the first event, he told himself yet again to forget about it.

'Don't let it get to you,' Sam whispered to himself. He knew what his tormentor was trying to do: unnerve and unsettle him, make him regret his decision to give up rugby, make him fail. But it wasn't going to work.

'Focus,' Sam said. He had to concentrate. All six disciplines, from the floor to the high bar, awaited him and Sam was going to have to demonstrate outstanding skill in every one of them. With several members of the national squad also competing, a high-placed finish would definitely bring him to the attention to the selectors.

There was a big crowd for the competition, the banked seating on each side of the sports arena virtually full. Somewhere up there sat Sam's parents and his sister, and Charlie too. A few school friends, including Ollie and other gymnasts from the club, were also there – all watching excitedly, all willing him to succeed.

But did they *all* want him to succeed? Was the Revenger there? Sam shook his head; he couldn't let the dark thoughts creep in again.

'Are you okay, Sam?'

Sam turned and saw Mike Thompson studying him closely.

'Why?' Sam said, more sharply than he intended.

'You look … a bit edgy. Are you nervous?'

'No more than I usually am.'

'Good lad.' Mike seemed reassured. He gazed up at the crowd. 'Quite a few people out there rooting for you today. Let's give them a good performance, eh?'

Sam nodded, feeling a new surge of determination. His family and his friends – real friends – were there to give him their full support. He wouldn't let them down. He would do his very best and nothing the mystery messenger could say or do was going to stop him.

'Let's go,' he said.

First, it was the floor exercise; Sam always enjoyed it. The combination of somersaults, twists and leaps, with rhythmic, almost dance-like movements, led some people to believe that it was the easiest of the six-event programme. Sam knew this was far from true. The floor exercise was tough and demanding. His programme lasted for a minute – sixty seconds in which he had to demonstrate his strength, flexibility and balance.

From the moment Sam sped gracefully into his first run and leapt into a twisting somersault, he felt the routine would go well. There were gasps from the audience at the height of his leaps and at the smoothness of his landings. He made full use of the entire floor area and finished the routine perfectly.

The audience burst into applause and as Sam waved and then ran from the floor, all thoughts of the texts and online threats had disappeared.

'Great work,' Mike said as Sam towelled himself down and other gymnasts gave him appreciative nods and pats on the back. 'You'll score well with that.'

Sam did score well. When the points were displayed, there were more gasps and applause. Sam was up with the leaders; it was great to make such a strong start.

Next was the pommel horse. It was another tough exercise. They were all tough exercises, but Sam was feeling on top form. He leapt onto the horse and slipped smoothly into the sequence of swings, leg circles and scissor movements. He moved all over the horse with growing confidence, never stopping and with hardly an error.

At the dismount he went high into the air and landed almost perfectly. When the marks came up he had scored highly again and was still up with the leaders.

'You're going well, Sam,' Mike told him as they waited for the next event and watched other gymnasts in action. 'As good as we could hope for.'

'I could have done better on that one,' Sam said.

'There's a long way to go. You know what's next, don't you?'

Sam turned to his coach and nodded. Of course he knew what was next. It was the most difficult event in men's gymnastics: the rings.

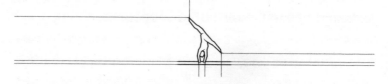

Sam was swinging round and round, high in the air, more than two-and-a-half metres above the floor.

This was the toughest discipline, especially for someone of Sam's age. His arm muscles screamed as his hands gripped the rings and his body moved back and then forward through a series of swings and holds.

It was so tough and so demanding, although part of the skill was to make it appear as though it took almost no effort at all. Sam had a powerful, muscular young body, but this event was a killer for even the strongest of gymnasts.

Sam silently told himself to stay relaxed. He was in a held-pike position – his body folded – and slowly and smoothly he came back and up into a handstand, with barely a movement from the rings.

He swept down into powerful swings and began to build speed towards his dismount, then he released the rings, twisted and turned in the air and landed with just the smallest step forward. He was annoyed about the tiny mistake, but it hardly spoiled another great effort.

The applause rang down from the watching spectators, but not all of it was for Sam. Elsewhere in the arena, other young gymnasts were demonstrating exactly why Great Britain had risen so high in the world rankings over the past few years. The positive signals for London 2012 and beyond were getting stronger and stronger.

Next for Sam was the vault, the event he and Mike had been practising in the school gym. Sam came pounding down the twenty-five metre runway, arms swinging high. His feet thumped down on the springboard, gaining great lift-off and perfect contact with the table, and he went flying into the tucked vault.

It was good, and this time – to both Mike's and Sam's delight – he did stick it on the landing.

Just two to go now, and up first were the parallel bars – Sam's favourite event, and his strongest too.

He was beginning to feel weary but the tiredness didn't show as he started his routine. His performance was inspired. Every move went like clockwork and as Sam made another perfect landing he smiled, thinking that even his tin acrobat couldn't have done better. Applause rang around the arena and when the points came up soon after, the cheers were even louder.

With just the gruelling high bar remaining, Sam was suddenly very tired – not just physically but emotionally, too. He felt drained. It had been a tough, tiring day at the end of a tough, tiring week.

As he waited for his turn on the bar, the memory of the texts suddenly flashed into his thoughts.

'Loser!' The word stuck in his mind. He shook his head, trying to force it away.

'No!' he said out loud, without even meaning to.

Mike was at his side. 'What?'

'Nothing,' Sam answered quickly.

'You all right?'

Sam nodded. 'Bit tired, that's all.'

'I'm not surprised, but we're nearly there. Stick with it.'

Sam nodded again. Mike was right. He just had to hold it together for a little longer. He shook his head again and forced away the troubling thoughts as he approached the high bar.

Sam dredged up his last reserves of strength and determination as he went through his final routine, demonstrating a good variety of forward and backward swings, turns, releases and re-grasps. It wasn't a perfect routine, and maybe it looked a little weary, but it was good. He finished with a spectacular dismount that he almost, but not quite, stuck.

A fantastic competition was at an end. When the final points were added up, Sam had finished in second place overall, beating two members of the national junior squad. And to top it all, his parallel bars score was the highest of the day.

Mike was grinning broadly as they waited for the medal presentation. 'Something tells me you'll be hearing from the national selectors very soon,' he said, thumping Sam on the back in congratulation. 'We're on our way!'

Twelve

Charlie stared at the text message.

> **Second!!! U r such a LOSER!!! An u thought it would get better soon. No, LOSER. Its gonna get much much worse!! U will C...**

'It usually ends like that, with some sort of threat,' Sam said. They were at Charlie's house. The competition had been so close to Sam's home town that he'd been given the rest of the weekend off.

'How long has it been going on?' Charlie asked. He looked furious.

'It started after the school lost the match I should have played in,' Sam replied.

'No one can blame you for a lost rugby match when you didn't even play in it.'

'Someone can, and does.'

Charlie read the text again. 'And you've no idea at all who's sending them?'

Sam sighed. 'The trouble is, the longer it goes on, the more I suspect almost everyone. The only person at school that I'm absolutely certain is innocent is Ollie, and once or twice, I've even suspected him.'

'But that's crazy.'

'I know it is. After you, Ollie's my closest friend. But when it keeps happening, texts and online, you start thinking stupid things.'

'Then you have to put a stop to it.'

'How can I do that when I don't know who it is?'

'Report it. Haven't you heard of zero tolerance? This is bullying – cyber bullying.'

'I wouldn't call it bullying, not really,' said Sam. 'Bullying is what happens to little kids in the playground.'

'Oh, Sam,' Charlie said. 'Bullying is exactly what this is. Tell someone at school, or your parents. Or the police.'

'No!' Sam said firmly. 'I have to sort this out myself. Whoever is sending me these messages reckons I'm a loser and a coward.'

'If you don't want to report it, then let me do it.'

'No, Charlie! I'm not a coward. I can deal with my own problems.'

Charlie's parents were out and he was making lunch. The house had been adapted to let him manoeuvre his wheelchair easily from room to room and around the kitchen so that he could cook. He handed Sam back his phone and went to the cooker. On the hob, water was starting to come to the boil, gently bubbling and swirling in the saucepan.

'Of course you're not a coward, Sam,' Charlie said, opening a bag of pasta. 'But you're not dealing with this the right way.'

Sam shrugged his shoulders. 'I'll find out who it is.'

'How?'

'Somehow. He'll make a mistake.'

'Or *she* will.'

Sam laughed. 'That's what Dr Watson says.'

'Who?'

'Ollie.'

'But his name's not—'

'He's playing Dr Watson in the school play – it's Sherlock Holmes. Ollie reckons he's quite a detective and he says it could be a girl, too. And he also says that we'll find out, somehow, who's doing this.' Sam's face darkened. 'And when we do—'

The phone in Sam's hand suddenly buzzed, interrupting his thoughts. Another text had arrived.

The two boys looked at each other and Sam took

a deep breath. He lifted the phone and pressed the button to open the text.

> **Hey LOSER, staying at home 2day? Maybe the Revenger will come an visit u. Would u like that??? Or maybe I'll wait til u get back 2 school. More surprises in store for u. Have a gr8 day LOSER!!**

More threats. Sam was burning with fury. Suddenly a spitting and sizzling sound came from the hob. The water had boiled over and was pouring down the side of the saucepan.

Thirteen

School assembly was not always the most exciting start to the day and by the time the headmaster was reading out the various notices, many of his pupils were fidgeting and restless, ready to move on to their first lesson.

On Monday mornings, the head usually had more to say than on any other day, and this Monday was no exception. There were announcements about special trips, after-school lessons, extra rehearsals for the school play, and all-important rugby results and fixtures.

The head's deep voiced droned down from the stage. Other teachers sat behind him, doing their best to appear interested. 'Finally...' he said, searching through the papers in his hands.

In the hall, Ollie sat next to Sam, a few rows back from the front. He gave him a gentle nudge with one elbow. 'At last,' he whispered.

'Shhhh,' Sam replied. Speaking during assembly could mean an after-school detention.

'Finally,' the head said again, having found the sheet of paper he was searching for. 'I want to make special mention of…' He glanced down at the paper. 'Sam Warder.'

Many faces turned to look towards Sam, some of them friendly and others hostile. Sam hadn't been expecting this, and didn't particularly want the attention, considering that right now he wasn't the most popular pupil in the school.

'Where are you, Sam?' the head called.

Slowly, Sam raised his right arm.

'Ah, yes, there you are. Stand up, please. Stand up.'

Reluctantly, Sam got to his feet, knowing that more than five hundred pairs of eyes were focusing on him.

It must have been Mike, Sam said to himself, wishing that his coach hadn't bothered.

With Sam standing there red-faced, the head spent the next minute describing how the star gymnast had done the school proud with his outstanding performance in the regional championships. Sam heard the voice, but not the words because his thoughts were elsewhere. He knew that one pair of eyes staring at him belonged to his tormentor and that this unwanted praise would probably lead to a fresh flood of texts.

'So,' the head's voice said loudly, 'let's all give Sam a very well-deserved round of applause.'

At Sam's side, Ollie clapped loudly enough for ten people. A few others nearby joined in with generous applause and the occasional cheer. Up on the stage, Mike Thompson was clapping so hard that it looked as though he might seriously damage his hands. Other teachers, including the rugby coach, Mr Farrow, clapped politely and smiled.

But in the rest of the hall, the applause was not just quiet, it was hardly there at all. And after a few seconds, the applause changed to a slow handclap. At first it was just a few pupils, but then it was picked up by more and more as the sound grew in volume.

Sam went an even brighter shade of crimson and sank down onto his chair, staring at the floor, totally embarrassed as the slow handclap echoed around the hall, getting louder and louder. Then, from somewhere, boos began to ring out.

Mike Thompson leapt to his feet, glaring furiously at the assembled pupils.

The headmaster looked stunned, for a few seconds. Then he shouted, loudly, 'Stop this! Stop this now!'

The room was instantly silent. Slowly, the headmaster craned his neck forward, his piercing eyes seeking out the ringleaders.

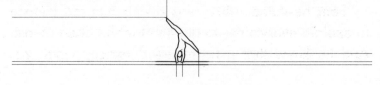

'What's going on, Sam?'

Sam shrugged his shoulders. 'I don't know.'

Mike's anger had not disappeared during the minutes it had taken to clear the hall at the end of assembly. 'I don't know if I believe that,' he said. 'Someone's got it in for you. The head is absolutely furious and so am I. He's asked me to look into it; find out exactly what's going on.'

Sam had never seen his coach look so angry. Mike was seething, pacing up and down outside the school hall.

'There's nothing to look into,' Sam said. He glanced at his watch. 'I ought to go, sir – I've got English first lesson.'

'Is this still about rugby? Is that what it is?'

'I suppose so. It's a rugby school and we lost a match that we should have won. Some people can't get over the fact that I quit the team.'

'Which people?'

'I don't know. Really, I wish I did. Then I could … speak to them.'

Mike looked at Sam closely. 'And … has anything else like this happened? Anyone confronted you, or threatened you? We can't just let this go, you know.'

Sam hesitated. Mike was giving him the chance to explain everything, to get it out in the open at last. And he knew that if he revealed exactly what was happening, the school staff would instantly sweep into action to seek out the culprit.

Part of him wanted to say, 'Yes, I'm being picked on, bullied, victimised, and I don't know how to deal with it. So help me, please.'

But Sam couldn't say that. He couldn't admit that he – a strong, fearless gymnast and athlete – was being bullied like a small child. And he couldn't say how helpless he felt and how much it was getting to him and how deeply it was hurting.

He smiled. 'No, there's nothing else, sir,' he said. 'And, if it's okay with you, I really should be getting off to English now.'

Fourteen

REVENGER was back online. Sam had known for certain that it would be only a matter of time after the display during assembly.

That evening, the request to chat came, and again Sam accepted it. But this time, he wasn't alone as he gazed at his laptop. Ollie was with him, staring wide-eyed as the words appeared one by one on the screen.

REVENGER: Not a very popular boy r u LOSER? I could have told u that. Did u like the slow hand clap? I started it.

Sam glanced at Ollie, and saw that his friend looked petrified. 'It's all right, Ollie,' he whispered, almost as though whoever was online could actually hear what he said. His hands went to the keyboard.

SAM WDR: U should feel proud of yourself.
REVENGER: Oh, I do. Sooooooooooo proud. The head didnt have a clue it was me.

SAM WDR: He'll find u. Or I will.

REVENGER: I dont think so!!!!!!!!!!!!!!!

SAM WDR: Wot do u want?

REVENGER: To chat. We're friends, aren't we?

SAM WDR: Are we?

REVENGER: Used 2 b. But then u used to have lots
of friends.

SAM WDR: I still have friends.

REVENGER: Dont think so!!!!!! Unless u r counting
that joker Ollie, but then hes a bit of a LOSER 2!

Ollie's eyes bulged. Sam was stunned too. But surely, whoever was online couldn't know that Ollie was in the room now. It wasn't possible. There was no webcam. 'He doesn't know you're here,' Sam said. 'He can't know.'

'I hope not,' Ollie said quietly. 'This is seriously spooky.'
Sam began to type again.

SAM WDR: Wot do u want? Why are you doing this?

REVENGER: I'm the REVENGER. I want revenge.

SAM WDR: You're pathetic. And when I find out who
you are, I'll

The cursor on the screen continued to blink, but no more words appeared because Ollie had grabbed Sam's hands and pulled them away.
'Don't! Don't threaten him!'

'Why not?' snarled Sam. 'I'm not scared of this creep.'

'No, but if you start threatening him, you're as bad as he is. That's what he wants. If you threaten him, then he wins. Stay calm, please.' Ollie looked seriously worried.

Sam sucked in a huge breath and then nodded. Ollie was right.

More words began to appear on the laptop screen.

REVENGER: U were saying? What stopped u?

SAM WDR: How long is this going to go on 4?

REVENGER: Until Ive had my revenge. Or maybe until u c some sense LOSER.

SAM WDR: You mean go back to rugby?

REVENGER: Would b a start. After that Id have 2 c.

SAM WDR: I'm not giving in to threats, from u or anyone.

REVENGER: Very brave, loser, but as u r a COWARD I think u will. Meantime, Ive set up something in ur honour.

'What does that mean?' Ollie said.

'I don't know,' Sam answered. 'But I think we're about to find out, and I don't think there'll be much honour about it.' He went back to the keyboard.

SAM WDR: Wot is it?

REVENGER: U could call it a little tribute site.

```
Ive worked v hard on it as Im sure u will agree.
Follow the link. Even a LOSER like u can do that.
I'll b back 2 c what u think but bye 4 now............
```

A blue-coloured link to a web address beginning with the word 'samisaloser' appeared on the screen.

'Don't click on it,' Ollie said quickly. 'There might be some sort of bug to destroy your laptop.'

'No,' Sam said, shaking his head. 'He wants me to see it, that's the whole idea. It's all part of the plan.' He clicked on the link and was quickly shifted to a website.

It was even worse than Sam had feared.

It began: *Sam Warder is a LOSER who let down his friends and his school. Sam Warder is a COWARD who gave up rugby because he was scared. This site is a tribute to Sam Warder.*

The site made grim reading and viewing, because as well as the cruel words and invented stories, there were fake photographs showing Sam on his knees or crying or running away or begging for mercy.

'Whoever is doing this, is really good at web design,' Ollie said.

'That lets you and me off the hook,' Sam replied. 'But half the people in this school could have done it. Someone must have snatched photos of me on a mobile phone.'

'Yeah,' Ollie answered, staring closely at the screen. 'Or maybe copied some from rugby team line-ups. And then put your head on someone else's body.' He pointed at one of the photos. 'I'm sure I've seen that photo of you somewhere.'

Sam shrugged and clicked on a section called 'Great Losers and Cowards in History'. Number one on the list was Sam Warder.

'Must have taken days,' Sam said. 'This guy really hates me.'

'It's getting dangerous. You've got to report it now.'

'No,' Sam said. 'And I don't want you reporting it either, or mentioning it to anyone else. I said exactly the same thing to Charlie.'

Ollie sighed and shook his head. 'It seems to me that we're the only sensible friends you've got.'

'Maybe,' Sam said. 'But he's not going to beat me.'

'Or she,' Ollie reminded him.

Sam took one last look at the site and then clicked off it and shut down his laptop. 'It makes me feel … horrible … just looking at it.'

'It is horrible,' Ollie agreed. 'And whoever's doing it should be thrown out of the school. But...' Ollie's voice trailed off.

'But?' Sam said. His friend looked very thoughtful.

'But,' Ollie said again, 'I think he or she might have left us a few clues this time.'

Fifteen

Despite his brave words, Sam was much more worried than he would admit to even his two closest friends. The website had taken the cyber-bullying to a more sinister level. Sam wasn't scared of his tormentor, but the constant threats and taunts were slowly but relentlessly attacking his confidence.

Sam kept seeing the faked photos in his mind. He kept remembering the words written in the last text or posted online. He found it difficult to sleep, which made him edgy and restless.

His worries began to show in class and after a few days he was called in to see the head of year.

Miss Pooley was one of the most popular teachers in the school. Being head of year, she was used to listening to pupils' problems, big and small, and she was good at spotting when a pupil had serious worries.

'A couple of your teachers have spoken to me, Sam,' she told him once he'd sat down in her office.

'They're a little concerned about you. They say you seem … distracted. Is there something worrying you?'

For a few seconds, Sam was again tempted to tell the truth. It would have been so easy to do. Miss Pooley was kind and considerate – all he needed was the strength to speak up.

But Sam was proud and stubborn. 'No, miss,' he said firmly.

Miss Pooley wasn't going to give up easily. 'I know gymnastics takes up a lot of your time. Could that be affecting your concentration in class?'

'Not at all. Concentration is part of gymnastics. I'm good at concentration.'

'And what about rugby?'

'What about rugby?'

Miss Pooley frowned. Anyone would have noticed that Sam's answers were brief and curt. It was unlike him; he was usually one of the most polite and friendly students in his year group. 'I understand you gave up playing for the school team recently?' the teacher said calmly.

'I had to choose between them,' Sam said.

'And you're still happy with the choice you made?'

'Of course.'

'What about your friends? Do they think you made the right choice?'

Sam hesitated. 'My real friends do. They understand.'

'But what about the booing and the slow handclapping in assembly the other day?'

'That was nothing,' Sam said quickly.

'Nothing? It couldn't have been very pleasant for you.'

Sam shrugged his shoulders. 'If a few people don't like the fact that I gave up rugby for gymnastics ... well, I just have to live with it.'

Miss Pooley smiled, as if realising that she wasn't going to get Sam to tell her the full story.

'Okay, Sam,' she said. 'We'll leave it there for now. But come and see me again in a week or so, will you?'

'But I'm okay, really.'

Miss Pooley nodded. 'I know you are. But come and see me, anyway. We can always talk about gymnastics.'

Sixteen

Detective Ollie was on the case. He told Sam that he had been making enquiries all over the school. His part in the school play as Dr Watson, had inspired Ollie to seek out his friend's tormentor. And Ollie reckoned that, just like Sherlock Holmes, he had solved the mystery.

Right now, the two boys were walking in the grounds. Nearby, on one of the rugby pitches, a match was underway, but Sam had decided that he would arrive midway through the game. That way, he told Ollie, everyone would be concentrating on the game, and his arrival would go unnoticed. At least, he hoped it would.

But Ollie had far more important matters than rugby to discuss. 'I've thought it through,' he said. 'I've looked at all the evidence.'

'What evidence?' asked Sam.

'Well, not exactly evidence, but clues, very strong clues. And after weighing everything up, I've worked it out and, as far as I can see, there's only one person it can possibly be.'

'Who?'

'Wait a minute,' said Ollie, clearly warming to his detective role. 'Let me tell you how I discovered the truth.'

'I'd rather you just told me who it is.'

Ollie ignored him. 'You remember when he...'

'Or she.'

'No,' Ollie said definitely. 'It's a "he", I know that now.'

'All right, *he*,' Sam said. 'Go on.'

'You remember that when he was online I said he'd left us clues? Well, he had.'

'Really?'

'Yes.' Ollie smiled. 'Firstly, he said that he *used* to be a friend of yours.'

'Half the school could say that.'

'Not really. Not close friends.'

Sam shrugged. 'Is that the best you've got?'

'Not at all, I'm just starting.'

'So get on with it, then.'

'Right, here's the real clincher,' said Ollie. 'You remember that the Revenger, as he calls himself, calls you a loser?'

'How could I forget?' Sam sighed.

'Well, he also called me a loser.'

'Did he?'

'Yes! He called me a joker, remember? Then he said that I was a bit of a loser too.'

'So?'

Ollie's face set hard. For once he wasn't his usual joking self. 'Someone we know has called me a loser before, quite a few times. In fact, he's insulted me fairly often. We just haven't taken it seriously until now.'

Sam stopped walking and turned to his friend. 'You mean Felix, don't you?'

Ollie nodded. 'It's him; he's behind all this. And there's more.'

'Go on,' Sam said, suddenly very serious.

'You said that he couldn't possibly have known that I was in the room the other day,' Ollie said excitedly. 'But what if he had only just left? Then he'd know, or he'd have a pretty good idea, that I was still there. Felix was in the room until just before our friend Revenger came online.'

Sam thought back. It was true; Felix had been there that day.

'Yes,' he said, reliving the moments in his mind. 'But … but Jack was there, too. And he'd only just gone.'

'It's not Jack!' Ollie snapped. 'It couldn't be Jack. He's just a sheep, doing what everyone else does and says. Jack wouldn't have the nerve to do something like this. Believe me, Sam. It's Felix.'

They were both silent. Ollie might be certain that Felix was the mystery cyber-bully, but Sam still wasn't so sure. For all his temper and his straight talking, Felix had been a good friend.

Suddenly the silence was broken by a buzzing noise. A text had arrived.

Sam hurriedly pulled the phone from his pocket and tapped the button to open the text.

> **Hey LOSER, not coming 2 the match??? U should b here. Its a disgrace and its all ur fault. U will be so sorry 4 this LOSER!!!!!!!**

Sam showed the message to Ollie and then snapped the phone off, glaring at his friend. 'So much for your detective work! It can't possibly be Felix, can it?'

'Why not?' said Ollie, looking bewildered.

'Because Felix is playing in the match! Do you think he's got his mobile phone on the field with him?' Sam stomped off towards the rugby pitch. 'Come on,' he called over his shoulder. 'We'd better see what's going on.'

Ollie chased after his friend. 'There's someone helping him!' he shouted. 'That's the only answer. He's got an accomplice!'

'Oh, shut up, Ollie!'

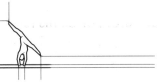

It was painful to watch. The Waterlands team was being hammered, bashed and battered towards the biggest defeat of the season.

The players out on the pitch couldn't entirely be blamed. The team was still missing a number of regulars, and the side they were up against was one of the best around. Even with Sam and the others in the home side, the visitors would have been very difficult to beat.

But this was embarrassing. Waterlands were losing 34–7 and there was still a good part of the second half to go. It looked as though this could end up as a record defeat.

There were several hostile glares as Sam and Ollie appeared, but most people were concentrating on the match and the humiliation being heaped on the home team.

'Hold them!' yelled a boy standing close to Sam and Ollie. 'Great tackle, Felix!'

Sam smiled, Felix had just made a great, try-saving tackle. 'Well done, Felix,' he muttered.

The boy turned to Sam. 'He's having a brilliant game. If it wasn't for Felix, we'd be at least another fifteen points down.'

Sam's smile grew wider. Whatever Ollie had decided, he didn't want to believe that Felix was the cyber-bully. And until someone proved otherwise, he wasn't going to believe it.

On the pitch, the ball broke free from a scrum, bouncing loose on the grass as players from both sides swooped towards it.

Felix was the fastest. He grabbed the ball and set off like a greyhound towards the opposing team's try line. Dodging and weaving, he avoided one tackle and then another.

'Go, Felix, go!' Sam couldn't stop himself from yelling. And he wasn't the only one – wild shouts and cheers rang along the touchline.

Felix had made such a quick break, there was no one to pass to; he had to go all the way on his own. Gasping for breath, he somehow made the last ten metres and dived over in one corner, touching down for the try.

The cheers from the touchline echoed around. At long last there was something to celebrate, and for the first time in what seemed like years to Sam, no one was casting hostile looks in his direction. Everyone was cheering.

But that was as good as it got for Waterlands. As the players tired during the final fifteen minutes, the other team ran in two more tries of their own. And both were converted.

At the final whistle, the score was 48–12 and Waterlands had slipped to its biggest defeat in years.

Sam and Ollie strode quickly away, anxious to escape the bitter looks and angry comments.

'I've been thinking,' Ollie said as they walked. 'It could still be Felix you know. He could have sent that text at half-time.'

Sam glared at his friend, then put his head down and kept walking.

Seventeen

Mike held the letter in his hand like it was something precious. He had read it through numerous times and had shown it to everyone at the club that evening, some of them twice.

The brief letter invited Sam to train with the UK junior gymnastics squad, exactly what both he and Mike had been hoping for.

But now that the invitation had arrived, Mike couldn't help feeling that he was more thrilled about it than Sam. The young gymnast was acting as if his mind was somewhere else.

Mike hadn't forgotten about the slow handclapping and booing in the school hall, but so far he had been unable to find the culprit. He wondered if this had something to do with Sam's troubled frown.

Sam went through his warm-up but even that, Mike thought, seemed sluggish.

First up in training that night was the high bar, which had been Sam's least successful event in the recent championships. His routine needed polishing and adapting slightly, but before starting work Mike needed to know that Sam was ready – both physically and mentally.

The coach carefully folded the letter of invitation and slipped it into his sports bag. 'Are you all right?' he said to Sam.

'Yes,' Sam replied sharply.

'Really? Are you sure?'

'Look, I'm fine. Why does everyone keep asking me if I'm all right? I'm just a bit tired, that's all.'

'I see,' Mike said. 'Do you feel unwell?'

'No.'

'Are you sure? We could see the school doctor, or your own doctor if you like?'

'I don't need to see a doctor.'

'Are you sleeping?'

Sam shrugged his shoulders. 'Not brilliantly. I go to sleep, but then I wake up in the middle of the night.'

'So what's on your mind? Not still the rugby, is it? Surely everyone's got over that by now?'

Sam sighed. 'I wish,' he said.

Mike looked closely at Sam, who suddenly seemed incredibly unhappy. 'Miss Pooley came to see me,' the coach said gently. 'She said that you'd not been your usual self in class. A few teachers—'

'*Two* teachers,' Sam corrected him.

'All right, two teachers had told her that you're not concentrating in class like you should. And two is enough. I'm a teacher too, remember?'

'I'm fine, Mike,' Sam said. 'I'm just a bit tired, that's all.'

Mike wasn't convinced. He followed Sam out to the high bar and watched as he jumped up and took a firm grip with both hands.

'Okay,' Mike said. 'Let's go through the routine once and then we'll think about possible changes. I've got a few ideas.'

Sam nodded, took a deep breath and began to swing his body, his arm muscles flexing.

He went into the routine, but Mike spotted in seconds that the boy looked far from relaxed. 'Sam, you don't look good,' he called. 'Come down and we'll talk it through and then start again.'

'I'm fine!' Sam shouted, swinging his way around the bar, building towards the first release and re-grasp, a manoeuvre that meant letting go of the bar completely and grabbing it again at the end of the move.

'Sam...' Mike breathed, not wanting to shout and distract the young gymnast, but knowing only too well that the move wasn't right. Sam swung under the bar and on the upward movement released his hold. His swinging motion took him over the bar as intended, but as his body flew downward it was obvious that he'd moved too far away to make the re-grasp. His fingertips just grazed the bar but got no hold at all.

Sam crashed into the padded mat with a loud slapping noise and all around the room other gymnasts turned to stare.

'Sam!' Mike yelled, racing over and crouching at Sam's side. The gymnast lay face-down.

'I'm okay,' Sam said. He was breathing hard but not moving.

'Are you sure? Nothing hurt?'

Ashen-faced and winded, Sam turned over and slowly sat up. 'Sorry,' he said. 'That was terrible. I'll do it again, once I get my breath back.'

'You will not do it again, not in this state.'

Sam looked up at his coach. 'What do you mean? What state?'

'You can't continue like this, Sam,' Mike said kindly. 'You have to tell me what's going on.'

Sam struggled to his feet. 'I told you, there's nothing going on.'

Mike was finding it hard to contain his anger. 'I don't believe you,' he said. 'Anyway, if you perform like this with the national squad, they'll send you straight back home. And you probably won't get a second chance.'

Eighteen

'I'd like to be considered for the school rugby team again, sir.'

Mr Farrow stared at Sam and for a few moments said nothing at all. 'I can't pretend I'm not surprised,' he said at last. 'You seemed so certain of your decision to give up rugby when we spoke before.'

'I … I was, then.'

'What's changed your mind?'

Sam had thought through this part of the conversation. He couldn't admit that he had finally given in to the constant pressure from his cyber-bullying tormentor. So the words he spoke next were true, but not the whole truth. 'I miss playing. I'd like to be in the team again.'

Mr Farrow got up from his desk, walked to the window and stared out. 'I'm not sure that it's as easy as that, Sam. You're a fine player and I won't say that the team hasn't missed you, because it has, very much.' He turned back from the window. 'But other people have stepped in when they were needed and they've performed to the best of their ability. I don't think I can ask them to stand down just because you've suddenly had another change of heart.'

'Oh,' Sam said. It hadn't occurred to him that he wouldn't walk straight back into the team after everything that had happened. 'No, of course. I don't expect anyone to stand down. But...'

'Yes?'

'Can I just make myself available for selection again? I mean, should a place in the team come up, I'd like to be considered.'

Mr Farrow nodded. 'Have you talked this through with Mr Thompson? He's mentioned to me about your invitation to train with the national squad and I'm really delighted for you.'

'But Mr Thompson knows that I've been unhappy about not playing rugby. I tried to see him before I came here, but he's not in school at the moment.'

'I see. And you didn't think you should wait until he's back and then speak to him first?'

Sam shrugged. 'I just wanted to get it done.'

'Is it really that urgent?'

'It... I...' Sam was struggling to find the words, without saying what was really troubling him. 'I thought the sooner the better.'

'And what about your fear of being injured?'

'I'm not going to worry about that. Not any more.'

Mr. Farrow paused before speaking again. 'Are you absolutely sure about this, Sam? There's nothing else bothering you?'

'No, there's nothing else, sir,' Sam answered, trying to look stronger than he felt. 'And I am sure. I want to play rugby again.'

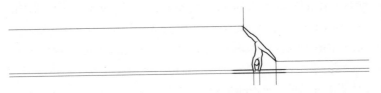

Sam was sitting on his bed, deep in thought, when Ollie walked into the room, closed the door and leaned back against it. He looked almost as miserable as Sam felt.

Ollie plodded over to a chair. 'Sometimes,' he said, sinking down, 'I think Sherlock Holmes didn't know what he was talking about.'

'What?' Sam said, barely looking up. His mind was still elsewhere.

Ollie was too deep in his own thoughts to notice. 'Sherlock Holmes said that when you eliminate the impossible, whatever remains, no matter how improbable, must be the truth.'

'*What?*' This time Sam did stare at his friend. 'What are you babbling on about?'

'Well, it was something like that.'

'What was?'

'What Sherlock Holmes said about the impossible and the truth.'

Sam raised his eyes to the ceiling. 'Ollie, I don't care what Sherlock Holmes or anyone else said.'

'But I do, I want to find out who's been threatening you,' said Ollie. 'I have to follow the clues so that I can eliminate the suspects one by one until I'm left with … with the truth.'

'And?'

Ollie sighed. 'I think I've eliminated *all* my suspects, so I've got no idea what the truth is.'

Despite his worries, Sam couldn't stop himself from smiling. 'Oh, Ollie,' he said, laughing, 'you're not such a great detective after all, eh? But it doesn't really matter now because—'

'No, listen,' Ollie interrupted. 'I went through everything that's happened and I narrowed my list of suspects down to three. There was, Sophie—'

'Sophie? Sophie Corbin?'

'Remember what she said to you at the match? About how she'd never forgive you?'

'She was just … angry. Like everyone else.'

'But she said it and I'd seen her glaring at you a couple of times, so she was on my list. But then…'

'Then?'

'She was really friendly to you yesterday, in history.

She wasn't angry at all. And it wasn't acting, because I know about acting.'

Sam smiled. 'She wasn't angry at me because Felix played well in the match and she's a lot more interested in Felix than she is in me.'

'Is she?' said Ollie, looking puzzled. 'Why?'

'Because she fancies Felix. She's liked him for ages.'

'Really? I didn't know that.'

'So much for the great detective.'

Ollie stood up and began pacing around the room. 'Anyway, I finally eliminated Sophie after history yesterday. Then there was Nick Thorrington. He called you a coward, which is one of the words the Revenger uses.'

'A lot of people have called me a coward.'

Ollie stopped pacing. 'But then I remembered that Nick came up to you and made a point of saying that he wasn't afraid of telling you to your face that you are a coward.'

'So why would he then text me, or tell me online…?'

'Exactly,' Ollie said, despondently. 'I thought maybe it was a double bluff, but Nick Thorrington's not bright enough for that. And he's useless on the computer – I've seen him in the library, always asking his friends for help. No, it's not him. And my only other suspect was Felix.'

'Oh, not Felix again.'

'It's not impossible if he has an accomplice.'

Suddenly, the door flew open and Felix came bursting into the room.

'I want to say that I'm sorry,' he said loudly to Sam. 'I should never have called you a coward.'

Ollie stared. 'I told you,' he breathed.

Felix ignored him. 'I know you're not a coward, Sam. You just made a mistake, a bad one. But now you've been man enough to admit it, and that takes a lot of courage. I always knew you had courage, really.'

'What's he talking about?' Ollie said to Sam.

'I've been trying to tell you,' Sam replied.

But Felix wasn't finished. 'I'd like us to be friends again,' he said, holding out his hand. 'I said some unpleasant things, but you know me. Sometimes I don't stop to think. But ... can we shake hands?'

Sam smiled as he stood up and took Felix's outstretched hand in his. 'Of course, we can,' he said as they shook on it.

Ollie was totally confused. 'What is going on?'

'Hasn't he told you?' Felix said, as though he had just noticed Ollie for the first time. I thought you'd have been the first to know.'

'Know what?'

'I did try,' Sam said to Ollie.

'He's coming back to rugby,' Felix said excitedly. 'Mr Farrow mentioned it to Dick Thorpe and now it's all over the school.' He turned back to Sam. 'You can have my place. I'll stand down from the team.'

'No!' Sam said quickly. 'No way. I'm glad we can be friends again, but I've got to earn a place in the team, however long it takes.'

Felix beamed. 'It'll take no time at all – you're the best player we've got.'

Sam was smiling too, relieved that the tension that had hovered over the room for so long was finally beginning to lift.

The only person not smiling was Ollie. Sam's news had left him even more worried than before.

Nineteen

Mike Thompson and Sam were walking near the playing fields. It was lunchtime, and on one of the pitches younger pupils were enjoying a game of touch rugby with no real tackles, just touch and pass.

A game of football was in progress on another pitch, with at least twenty players on each side charging backward and forward after the ball. Even further away, a small group of pupils were on a hockey pitch, being coached in the skills of short and long corners.

Sam knew Mike was disappointed that he was going back to rugby, but his coach wasn't making a fuss.

'We'll try to make rugby and gymnastics work and see how it goes for a while,' Mike said. 'And we'll keep our fingers crossed that you can avoid injuries.'

Sam was surprised but relieved at this. His nerves were frayed and he wasn't sure that he could take much more questioning from Mike, or from anyone. 'Thanks,' he said softly, without looking at his coach. 'I'll do my best for you, I promise.'

'Do your best for yourself, Sam,' Mike replied. 'That's all I want.'

'It's still gymnastics first,' Sam said quickly. 'A place in the Olympic squad is what I want more than anything.'

But that wasn't quite true. Because more than anything, Sam wanted the cyber-bullying to go away. And for the past twenty-four hours it had seemed as though his plan was working. There had been no more texts and no more online contact. Perhaps it was truly, finally over.

Mike began talking about the training schedule and what Sam could expect when he joined up with the national junior squad. But Sam's thoughts were clearly still elsewhere.

The coach stopped walking and gazed around at the grounds. 'We're lucky at this school, aren't we?' he said. 'We have all these facilities and so many different sports: rugby, hockey, football, cricket and athletics...'

'I guess so,' Sam answered.

'But your sport – gymnastics – is different from all those others. Do you know why?'

Sam frowned. 'I'm not sure what you're getting at.'

Over on the football pitch, two young boys were tearing after the ball as it bounced towards the touchline.

'In all those other sports,' Mike said, 'it's team versus team or one against one. Gymnastics is different. There's no race, no match – just you, demonstrating your skills.'

On the football pitch, the ball suddenly flew high into the air and bounced towards them. Mike went to boot it back to the young footballers. But he was long out of practice as a footballer and as he kicked the ball it sliced off his shoe and span away in completely the wrong direction.

The pupils laughed and cheered and even applauded.

'Rubbish, sir!'

'Better stick to gymnastics!'

'Or science!'

Mike laughed and put his hands up. 'Sorry!' he yelled. Even Sam was smiling.

'All sport is wonderful,' Mike said to Sam. 'And ours is a beautiful sport. Don't ever forget that.'

The Waterlands rugby team had its next match – an away game against old rivals – on the following Saturday and Mr Farrow had already told Sam that he wouldn't be selected.

Sam didn't mind. He was training in the gym and at the club with Mike and most importantly there had been no more texts. Slowly but steadily, Sam was beginning to feel just a little more relaxed.

Ollie said very little about Sam's decision to go back to rugby. He just told Sam that he was going to keep looking for the cyber-bully, whether he liked it or not.

On the Friday morning, Sam was called in to see Mr Farrow. He hurried down to the rugby coach's office, expecting to hear that he should turn up to the training session the following week. But there was a surprise in store.

'Sam, I want you to play tomorrow after all,' said Mr Farrow.

'Tomorrow? But I thought...'

'Don't worry, no one is giving up their place for you. Tom Patterson has to go home this evening – his grandfather is unwell. So I want you to play at centre, alongside Felix. He had a very good game last time.'

Sam nodded. 'Yes, I saw him. He was excellent.'

'So let's see what sort of partnership you two can form, eh?'

The exciting news that Sam was back on the team had spread around the school by lunchtime. In the dining hall, he and Ollie were sitting side-by-side on one of the long tables when Felix came hurrying over with his own lunch.

He sat down facing Sam, grinning broadly. 'I'm really looking forward to playing with you.'

'Me too.' Sam smiled.

'I'm sorry about Tom's grandad, but I've heard it's not too serious. Tom should be back on Monday.'

'That's good.'

'We'll score one for him, eh?'

They spoke about the match for a while and then Felix remembered that he was late with some coursework, so he left to get it finished.

Ollie went too. The first night of the school play was fast approaching and the head of drama was squeezing in extra rehearsals whenever possible.

Sam was sitting alone, thinking about the following day's match, when he suddenly felt his mobile phone vibrate. There had been no more threatening texts since he'd gone back to rugby and Sam was gradually getting used to not feeling worried every time a new one arrived.

A little earlier, he had texted his sister and he smiled as he took out his phone, anticipating Emily's reply. But the smile instantly disappeared as Sam saw the mystery number. He opened the message.

Hey LOSER, didnt think
Id gone away did u???
Its a disgrace u r
back in the team. Im
getting 2 u, right???
U gave in but u r still
a COWARD. U will b
SORRY 4 all u have done.
So so sorry LOSER!!!!!!

Twenty

Mr Farrow always encouraged pupils to look at and enjoy the framed photos and rugby shirts that lined the walls of his office. He was proud of the school's history and tradition.

But Ollie had been studying the photos for a good twenty minutes as he tried to make out the faces.

Mr Farrow looked up from a mountain of paperwork and checked the clock. He was anxious to catch up with the rugby team and members of staff who had already left by coach for the away match.

'Are you going to be much longer, Ollie?'

'No, sir,' Ollie replied without looking away from the photographs.

'Good, because I'm leaving in another five minutes.'

'Oh, don't let me hold you up, sir. I'm fine.'

'I'm surprised you're not coming to the match,' Mr Farrow said. 'You usually do.'

'Can't, sir. Extra play rehearsal today. And you know I've got one of the leading roles.'

Mr Farrow smiled as he went back to his paperwork. 'I had heard.'

Ollie was doing everything he could to seek out new evidence in his hunt for the cyber-bully. He was determined to be thorough, just like Sherlock Holmes. He felt certain that he had seen one of the images the Revenger had posted on the website before. So he was searching through the framed rugby photos to see if it was there. Even if he found the photo, he wasn't sure what use it would be, but it might offer a clue.

Picking out Sam in the team line-ups was simple enough, but it took much longer for Ollie to find what he was really searching for – a great action shot of his friend running with the ball.

'That's it,' Ollie said at last. 'That's the one.'

Mr Farrow looked up again. 'What is?'

'Er … this photo of Sam. I think I might have seen it somewhere else.'

'You probably have.'

'Really?'

'It's on the school website.'

Ollie nodded. 'So that's how he did it.'

'Did what?'

'Oh, nothing, sir,' Ollie said, thinking that the Revenger would have copied the photograph from the school website and pasted it on the site he created. 'Simple, really. I should have realised.'

Mr Farrow looked up again. 'Do you always talk to yourself like this?'

Ollie grinned. 'Quite often, sir. I've usually got so many interesting things to say.'

Ollie was about to turn away from the photographs when his gaze was caught by another team line-up. It was an old photograph and Ollie stared when his eyes settled on not one but two faces he recognised. He moved in closer, studying the photo intensely, and then he read the names listed beneath.

'I've just noticed this photo of you, sir,' he said. 'You haven't changed a bit.'

'Very funny, Ollie,' Mr Farrow answered. 'I had a lot more hair then. And you don't need to remind me that it's a long time since I was a pupil at this school.'

Ollie's eyes were fixed on the other face. His eyes flicked downward and he looked again at the name at the bottom. 'This A. J. Richards, sir. Is he anything to do with Jack Richards? He looks just like him.'

'Yes, it's his father,' Mr Farrow said, standing up and walking over to Ollie. The teacher bent down and studied the photo. 'Yes, that's Tony Richards. He was a good player – hard as nails, but a bit hot-headed at times. If someone tackled him hard, he always made sure that he tackled them even harder as soon as he got the chance. We gave him a nickname.' He stared at the photo again, his brow furrowing as he tried to remember. 'What was it, now?'

Ollie's heart was thumping in his chest and his mouth was dry. He swallowed. 'It wasn't … Revenger, was it, sir?'

Mr Farrow turned slowly to Ollie. 'Yes, that's it. Revenger Richards, that's what we called him. How on earth did you know that?'

Twenty-one

Slotting back into the team wasn't proving quite as easy as Sam had hoped. His usual position was scrum-half. Close to the scrum, he was always in the thick of the action, the link between the forwards and the backs, making everything tick.

Today, he was inside-centre and it felt totally different. Here in the centre, it was more of a waiting game – waiting to be part of a running attack or waiting to fly into the tackle when the opposition backs began a run of their own.

It was a little frustrating for Sam, and on top of that, the forwards were dominating the game so far. The ball had hardly reached either set of backs – their shirts and shorts were almost as mud-free as when they put them on.

Sam was raring to make an impression. His chance came when an opposition player's downfield kick went straight into touch for a throw-in. The two sets of forwards lined up, waiting to leap high in their attempts to grab the ball.

Sam waited with Felix outside him, both knowing that this could be the chance for their first real attacking run.

The ball was thrown in, the forwards jumped and one managed to nudge it back to the Waterlands scrum-half, who swiftly moved it inside to the fly-half. The backs were away on a run at last.

The fly-half made excellent ground, neatly avoiding a tackle. He jinked and dodged and then sent a spinning pass to Sam who was now running at full speed.

Taking the ball safely in both hands, Sam hurtled towards the try line. The speed of the attack had taken the opposition backs by surprise and as Sam swerved past his opposite number and the field opened up, it looked as though he would be in for the try.

Felix was running at Sam's side, keeping pace, ready for the pass should it come his way. But that was unlikely – there was only one player to beat and it didn't look as though he would get close enough to Sam to attempt a tackle.

The try line was less than ten metres away and there was little danger from the final defender. Sam was heading for a great try. But at the last moment, he glanced to his left and passed the ball into the waiting hands of Felix, who charged over the line and touched the ball down.

He turned to Sam, beaming. 'You could have scored yourself. You gave that one to me!'

Sam smiled.

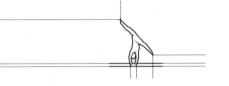

Ollie was pacing anxiously backward and forward, his mind racing, his thoughts tumbling. Like Sherlock Holmes, he had solved the crime and discovered the identity of the villain!

It was Jack. Shy, reserved Jack – the one person Ollie had not suspected – had to be the cyber-bully who'd been tormenting Sam for all this time. The clues were finally slotting together for Ollie, like pieces of a giant jigsaw puzzle.

Jack had never been around when Sam received the threatening texts or emails. Jack had been part of the crowd shouting and jeering at Sam at the rugby match, even though he'd kept himself in the background. And now Ollie thought about it, he was also pretty sure that Jack had been sitting where the booing and handclapping had started in the school assembly. Most convincing of all was the new finding that Jack's dad had been known as 'Revenger'.

But there was one question still deeply troubling Ollie. 'Why?' he said aloud. 'Why has he been doing this?'

Ollie shook his head, unable to answer his own question. And there was another problem to be solved. Ollie knew that he should report his findings to someone at school, but Sam had told him that this was something he alone would deal with if ever they discovered the identity of the Revenger.

'But what could Sam do on his own?' Ollie said to himself as he paced. 'And what should I do now?'

Finally, he made a decision. He picked up his mobile, scrolled through the list of numbers, found the one he was looking for and pressed the call button.

He placed the phone to one ear and listened. 'Answer the call,' he whispered. 'Please answer the call.'

After five rings, a voice finally answered. 'Hello?'

'Charlie, it's Ollie. You know, Sam's friend?'

'Yes, of course. Your number's on my phone from the other Saturday. Is everything okay?'

'Yes. Well, no. Not really.'

'Nothing's happened to Sam?'

'No, he's fine,' Ollie said quickly. 'But I've found out who it is…'

'What?'

'The Revenger. I know who it is, for certain. At least, I'm pretty certain. It can't be anyone else after what I've discovered.'

Swiftly, and as briefly as was possible for Ollie, he told Charlie how he had found out that the Revenger was a name given to Jack's father when he was a pupil and a star rugby player at the school.

'It has to be him,' Ollie said after revealing all the facts. 'He's used his Dad's nickname. But I don't know why he's got it in for Sam so badly. He doesn't even play rugby.'

'Maybe that has something to do with it,' Charlie answered.

'The thing is,' Ollie said, finally getting to what was really worrying him, 'I don't know what to do now that I'm sure it's Jack.'

Charlie didn't hesitate. 'You have to go and report it to someone at school. Now.'

'But Sam doesn't want me to tell anyone. And he said that he told you the same thing.'

'He did, but what Sam wants doesn't matter any more,' Charlie said firmly. 'Go and report it, Ollie. Go now.'

The match was drawing to an end and with the Waterlands team on top form, the threat of another heavy defeat had long disappeared. With just ten minutes to go, they were nine points ahead. Sam had played his part to the full, and was enjoying his return to rugby.

But with every minute that ticked by, he became more certain of one thing: rugby was fun but for Sam, gymnastics meant so much more. It was his dream and he wanted to live his dream. His thoughts were so much clearer now – maybe being out on the field had helped him face up to his own doubts and fears. After the match, he planned to speak to Mike Thompson and Miss Pooley to explain exactly what had been going on. They would root out the cyber-bully and put an end to his activities once and for all.

The home side's supporters were still urging their team on, but on the touchline the Waterlands supporters were noisily chanting for the victory.

Sam glanced in their direction and was surprised to see the two people he had been thinking about striding towards the supporters. Sam stared. Why were Mike and Miss Pooley here? He watched as they reached the group of supporters. Miss Pooley spoke to one of them and after a few moments a boy emerged from the group. He turned and Sam saw his face.

'Jack,' he whispered.

As Sam looked on, totally confused, he saw his roommate escorted away by the two teachers.

'*Sam!*'

Sam looked around, suddenly remembering that he was on the rugby pitch. And as he turned, he realised the reason for the shout. The ball was bouncing towards him, closely followed by two huge opposition forwards.

All three players lunged towards the ball in a jumble of arms and legs and somehow Sam's right hand touched the ground rather than the ball. Unable to stop his run, one of the big forwards trod heavily on Sam's hand and he screamed in agony.

The next second, a huge thigh thumped into the side of Sam's head and he went sprawling to the ground.

And then it all went dark.

Twenty-two

The atmosphere in the headmaster's office was tense and strained. All eyes were on Jack. His face was pale, his eyes were red and his cheeks were streaked with dried tears.

The headmaster, Mike Thompson and Miss Pooley sat on one side of the large desk; Jack and his dad were opposite.

For a short while, Jack had tried to deny his actions, but soon admitted everything: the texts, the online threats, the website, the slow handclaps in assembly. It all came spilling out.

Now Jack looked completely drained, as if his confession had left him exhausted. Jack's dad was just as pale but looked stunned too, as though he couldn't believe what he had heard.

The headmaster sighed heavily. 'You've admitted everything you did, Jack,' he said gently, 'and I'm glad about that. But you haven't told us why you did it.'

Jack stared at the floor.

'Jack?' the headmaster prompted. 'We really do need to know.'

Slowly, Jack lifted his head. Still avoiding eye contact, he spoke quietly and nervously. 'I … I always wanted to be good at rugby, like my dad, but I'm not.'

'That doesn't matter, Jack,' his dad said. 'I never—'

'Mr Richards,' the headmaster said firmly. 'We must let Jack speak.'

Mr Richards nodded.

'Dad never said anything about me being useless at rugby, but he was such a star when he was here. I wanted to be like him. And I tried, I really did, but … I was scared when I played rugby. Of being hurt. I've never told anyone, but I was frightened.' He fell silent for a moment. 'I'm sorry, Dad,' he said, still without looking at his father. 'I know that makes me a coward, but…'

'Jack—' said Mr. Richards.

'No, I want to finish,' Jack said, finally looking up. 'I was so angry when Sam gave up rugby. He's so good at it – brilliant – and he just gave it up. It wasn't fair. He had all that skill and he just threw it away. So I decided to make him suffer for it. And once I started, I couldn't stop. I wanted to hurt him more and more, in the only way I could.' He looked down at the floor again and spoke quietly, almost in a whisper. 'I was good at it.'

The room was silent for a few moments as everyone took it what Jack had told them.

'There's no shame in being scared,' Mr Richards said at last.

'You never were,' Jack answered, without looking up.

'But of course I was. And I still am scared sometimes. Everyone is.'

'But I was a coward.'

Mr Richards nodded. 'You were,' he said sadly. 'But not on the rugby field. You've been cowardly in what you've done to Sam. We're going to do everything we can to put that right. And then you're going to have to make a new start.'

Jack looked at the headmaster. 'Will I have to leave Waterlands, sir?'

'I'm afraid so,' the headmaster replied. 'You know the school has a zero-tolerance policy towards any form of bullying. And that goes for everyone.'

'I know. In a way I'm glad everyone knows now. I'm glad it's over. And I am sorry.' Tears were forming again in Jack's eyes. 'I really am so sorry.'

The headmaster sighed again. 'Yes. Yes, I believe you are.'

Jack wiped away the tears and swallowed hard. 'How is Sam?' he asked. 'Have you heard from the hospital?'

The headmaster looked over at Mike, who had returned from A&E a little earlier.

'He's awake,' Mike said. 'The doctors think he has a mild case of concussion, nothing to worry about. But his hand…' The gymnastics coach shrugged his shoulders. 'He's going for X-rays. We just have to hope that the injury is not too serious.'

Twenty-three

FOUR MONTHS LATER

The arena was buzzing with excitement. Everyone – spectators, coaches, and most importantly, the gymnasts – knew how important these national championships were. With the London 2012 Olympic Games just around the corner, a top finish was vital if gymnasts were to impress the selectors. And the leading juniors were fully aware that an outstanding performance could still mean a move into the senior squad and maybe, just maybe, a place in the Olympic team.

The standard was so high. The world-class gymnasts brought gasps of admiration and bursts of applause from the spectators – this was gymnastics at its very best.

Sam felt calm and relaxed; there were few nerves. His points so far meant that he was in with a chance of first place in the overall junior event. Every discipline had gone even better than he could have hoped. Floor, pommel, rings and vault ... all had been terrific. He'd pulled off every manoeuvre and stuck every landing.

As he waited for his next event, Sam looked down at his hands. The right one ached slightly, but that was to be expected. The studded boot that had crunched down on it had made its mark. Two small bones had been broken, causing fears of permanent damage.

But Sam was young and had received good treatment. The bones had mended quickly and it looked as though there would be no long-term problems.

Sam smiled and rubbed his right hand. It was a reminder to him of all that had happened in the previous months. Up in the stands his family and his two best friends, Charlie and Ollie, were all looking on. For a moment Sam thought of Jack, and couldn't help feeling a little sorry for him. But that was all over now. There had been no more threatening texts or online messages, and the website had been taken down. It was all just a bad memory.

Sam stood up; the parallel bars were next. He looked up. Mr Farrow and most of the rugby team, including Felix, were somewhere up in the stands, too, all rooting for the school's star gymnast.

Mike stood nearby. 'Focus,' he said softly to Sam. 'Concentrate.'

Sam nodded; he hardly needed telling. He looked at the parallel bars and it occurred to him that he had been trying to live parallel sporting lives – rugby and gymnastics – over the past few months.

He turned to Mike. 'Parallel lines can never meet.'

'What?' Mike asked.

Sam smiled and shook his head. 'Nothing. Let's go.'

He approached the bar and waited for the signal to begin. When it came, Sam was up onto the bars and into his routine in one flowing, liquid movement. He was grace and beauty, combined with strength and power as he swept through the mix of swings and holds above and below the bars.

The spectators fell silent, as if realising that they were watching one of the greatest displays of the entire championships.

As Sam built to the dismount, totally in control, Mike's words flashed through his mind. 'Ours is a beautiful sport. Don't ever forget that.'

Sam knew gymnastics was a beautiful sport and he would never forget what he had learned. He released the bars, soared high, twisting and spinning, and then stuck the landing like glue.

All around the arena, spectators were on their feet, cheering and applauding as Sam bounced from the mat. He felt fantastic, so fantastic that he wished he could finish with his famous running-up-the-wall trick. But he had to wait calmly for the judges' scores. And when they came, the score confirmed what Sam already knew. The dream was on. London 2012 beckoned.

Parallel lines

Blessed with twin talents, Sam Warder appears to have it all. A lightning fast scrum-half on the rugby pitch, he also performs feats of strength and agility on the parallel bars. But the London 2012 Games are approaching and Sam is at a crossroads. Flying in the face of peer pressure, he choos Gymnastics as his sport. And then the threatening text messages begin... Can Sam hold fast to his Olympic odyssey in a school where rugby is a religion?

ISBN 978-1-84732-750-5 • £5.99

Running in her shadow

A gifted track and field athlete, Megan Morgan has all the makings of an Olympic superstar. Whether sprinting, jumping or hurdling, her body moves like quicksilver and her sporting dreams look set to become realit Backing Megan all the way is her determined mother. A promising athle in her youth, she will not rest until her daughter competes for Team GB. E where is the line between love and obsession? And how much pressure can Megan withstand?

ISBN 978-1-84732-763-5 • £5.99

Available September 2011

Wheels of fire

Rory Temu is unstoppable on his battered BMX. Weaving and dodging though the Edinburgh streets there's no obstacle he won't tackle. Such brilliance on a bike could take Rory far – maybe even to th Olympic Games, so his teacher believes. But a gang on the streets has been watching too – and the members have their own plans for Rory's talents. Rory has a gift and he knows it, but can he keep his balance over such rough terrain?

ISBN 978-1-84732-813-7 • Publishing September 2011 • £5.99

Deep waters

Lucy Chambers lives to swim. Tipped as a potential Paralympian, she has watched the Aquatics Centre rise up near her London home and hopes to make a real impression there in 2012. But the ripples of Lucy's success have reached her mother, Sarah, who rejected her soon after she was born Both mother and daughter share a passion for swimming – but is now the right time to start sharing each other's lives? For Lucy, the waters have never been deeper...

ISBN 978-1-84732-764-2 • Publishing September 2011 • £5.99